PAINTED LADIES

OF
CINNAMON HOLLOW

E. C. HERBERT

For information contact: info@outlawspublishing.com

Cover Design by Outlaws Publishing LLC
Published by Outlaws Publishing LLC
July 2024
10987654321

Prologue

When the third mutilated, nude body of one of the town's Painted Ladies was found, Sheriff Tom Evers knew something was happening that he had never experienced before.

There was a serial killer on the loose.

This third body, one of Big Rear Rosy's girls was found behind the livery stable in the town known as Cinnamon Hollow, named after the first woman to arrive, when the town was just starting.

Not only was the town named after her, she was also the first mayor and owner of the Cinnamon Saloon and Boarding House. Cinnamon's sister Rose ran one of the town's three brothels.

This dead woman was one of Rosy's Roses, as they came to be referred to. Rosy's Roses were the top of the line girls and their cribs were larger than normal and well decorated.

They were well versed in the dance of love and encouraged to read the local paper to keep up on current affairs of the town and surrounding area. They had to keep up their appearance and bought fancier, frillier dresses than the girls from the other brothels in Cinnamon Hollow.

This was the second Rose to be killed.

The first was one of Magnificent Millie's girls.

The third Brothel, if you wanted to call it that, was at the edge of town and run by a Chinese lady, Sing Lin. It was just several tents set up acting as cribs for the girls who worked there.

Sing Lin had the cheapest, youngest girls, but they were pretty nasty in hygiene and dress and would service anyone.

None of Sing Lin's girls had been harmed yet.

With this new killing, Sheriff Evers told Cinnamon he was going to contact the office of the US Marshals for assistance.

US Marshal Harry Finch was contacted by the home office and was assigned the case. Kissing his new bride Amanda good-bye, Harry boarded the stage for Cinnamon Hollow, in what was to be an intriguing case.

Chapter 1

When the third nude, mutilated body was discovered behind the livery stable, Sheriff Tom Evers knew that something was happening that would demand more than he was capable of. So a telegram was sent out to Washington, DC to the Bureau of the US Marshals.

Cinnamon Hollow fell under the territory of US Marshal Harry Finch, so after he received a telegram from the main office, he was on a stage headed to Cinnamon Hollow.

This was the first case he had been assigned to since he had closed his Washington DC office and relocated to Thunder Point where Harry had met, and married, Amanda Wilson who he fell madly in love with, while working an earlier case.

It was difficult for both of them, that morning. This would be their first time apart since they were married, and already it seemed too long.

In the past when on assignment, Harry would be gone until he had solved and completed his assignment, which was his plan here except he never had someone back home waiting for him. This would be his first and he was missing her already.

The second thing Harry was missing already was his private rail car for traveling and he made a mental note;

when this case was over, to talk to Amanda about moving to someplace that was accessed by the railroad.

He recalled she was pretty adamant about staying in Thunder Point, but maybe if she was missing him like he was missing her, she would change her mind if he suggested it, but that was a discussion for later once he returned.

Inside the stage, which was occupied by a middle aged couple and a young, attractive woman dressed like she was headed for the dance hall, which was exactly where she was bound. It was an extremely hot day, mostly because the window flaps had been dropped in an attempt to keep out the dust that was kicked up from the dry road.

The gentleman, like Harry, had beads of sweat on his forehead, where the two women had nothing.

'How is it that a woman never sweats?' Harry asked himself. 'Dressed like they are, in layers of petticoats laced tightly around their bodies. A brassier also laced tightly and all covered by a layer of frilly material.'

Those thoughts made him even hotter, so he undid his tie, removed his jacket and taking a hankie from his pant's back pocket, wiped the sweat from his brow.

Having ridden in silence for a while and curious as to who Harry was sharing the stage with, he extended his hand toward the gentleman and introduced himself.

"Hello. I'm US Marshal Harry Finch," Harry said, waiting for his hand to be grasped in return of his introduction.

"I'm Benjamin O'Connor from the O'Connor Clan and this is my wife Catherine O'Connor."

Benjamin's handshake was firm, which told Harry something about his character.

'You can tell a lot by a man's handshake,' Harry thought, returning the firm grasp on his hand, then releasing it to offer it to Catherine, who, with her small, dainty hand simply touched his.

Even before Harry could remove his hand, it was taken by the other stage rider, the young, attractive woman.

"I'm Della DuPont, Marshal," she offered before Harry could. "Pleased to meet you." Her handshake was typical coming from a young woman.

Harry didn't know if she was expecting him to lean forward and to kiss that hand, but he didn't.

"Please to meet you to, ma'am," was all Harry offered.

Having introduced himself, he decided to make some small talk so that the time would go by faster and to not sit and concentrate on the heat. He would have to get out of the coach soon. Raising the window covering for a moment, Harry saw it was still too dusty to leave them open.

"So, tell me Benjamin O'Connor, what brings you to the midwest?" Harry asked.

"Well, lad, me and the misses are headed for California to our daughter's wedding next month, and decided to leave early so we could see parts of this great country," he told Harry. "Our daughter is a school teacher and she moved to California last year and fell in love with a male teacher and they are getting married."

Just then, all hell seemed to break loose inside the coach as a rear wheel dropped into a rut in the road and the spokes shattered sending the stage onto its axle and sending them all flying toward the back of the coach, where they landed all bunched together. Moments passed before the stage door opened and they were all helped out.

"Sorry folks," the driver said. "It will be a short time to put on another wheel. In the meantime, make yourselves comfortable over in that shade," he said, pointing to a large tree.

Harry heard the rattle of the snake, but not in time.

Mrs. O'Connor had gone to sit on a rock where a rattlesnake was curled up, enjoying the shade. She didn't see the snake and it struck out and bit her on the hand. Her blood curdling scream could be heard echoing through the hills, along with the "boooom" from Harry's forty-five, which blasted the rattler.

"With her husband at her side, Harry quickly took his pocket knife out and explained to them both what he needed to do. Benjamin held his wife's hand while Harry cut a line connecting the two puncture wounds. With that done, he put his mouth over this area and sucked as hard as he could, hopefully drawing out most of the snake venom. This he did several times.

"The next couple of days will be rough," Harry told him. "But I think we acted quick enough to have gotten most of the venom out, so at least her life would be spared."

Benjamin took off his coat and tore the sleeve of his shirt to make a bandage which he wrapped around her hand. A hug from her and a handshake from him was Harry's thanks that day.

It felt good to be outside in the air after the hot interior of the coach, but soon the wheel was replaced and they were once again under way. The afternoon heat again made the interior of the coach almost unbearable.

Once underway, Harry again started up a conversation, this time with the young lady, Della DuPont.

"So, Miss DuPont," he started to say, then felt he needed to clarify. "You are a Miss, I presume?"

"I am, Marshal, but I have had my share of proposals. All from drunken cowboys who thought a few minutes of bliss and lying next to a warm woman constituted love and marriage."

Even though she wore a smile, Harry picked up a little sadness in her voice.

"Well, I'm sure Miss DuPont, when the right guy comes about, I'm sure you will know it. But now, what is your destination?" he asked her.

"Thank you for the words of encouragement, Harry. You don't mind me calling you Harry, do you?"

"Not at all," he told her, noticing for the first time the coldness in her eyes, even though her voice and facial expressions were warm and inviting."

"I'm headed to Cinnamon Hollow where I will work as a dancer and singer for a Miss Rosy O'Neil. I answered an ad in our Daily Star newspaper that she was looking for professional women to work for her. I answered her ad and, wa'la! Here I am." She acted out her wa'la with hand expressions.

"Now you. Where are you headed?"

"I'm also headed for Cinnamon Hollow," Harry told her. "I have some business to attend to there."

"Maybe our paths will cross there and you can come and hear me sing, buy me a drink or dinner, even."

As inviting as that sounded to Harry, he knew who she was outside of being a singer and a dancer, and if there was a killer in Cinnamon Hollow targeting the town's Painted Ladies, she would be a new target, being a new arrival.

Harry saw that both of the O'Connor's had fallen asleep.

'That's good she is sleeping,' thought Harry. 'Sleep being the best healer. And Benjamin looking so worried and concerned as I sucked the poison from her body. True love.' He concluded in his mind, 'Just as I would feel for Amanda, if I was in your shoes.'

"Harry, Harry," a far away voice echoed in his head. "Harry, Harry."

Harry was brought back to the present by Della's voice.

"Sorry. I was just thinking of my wife and for as much as your offer for drinks or dinner, I have to refuse you now."

Harry knew that as long as he didn't put himself in any compromising position with another woman, he would be okay. After all, he was a newly married man and madly in love with his Amanda.

"I'm sorry to hear that, Harry. It sounds like you feel I might have a different reason for suggesting drinks or dinner, but trust me I don't."

Harry knew that if there was a killer of prostitutes in Cinnamon Hollow, Della sure would be a good target, not knowing anyone there and being a singer and a dancer she would be very public and in a short period of time, everyone would know her.

The stage had slowed some, so Harry pulled open one of the window flaps, and not being confronted with a face full of dust, rolled it completely open letting in the cooler, afternoon air.

Once Harry saw that the dust had died down he continued to roll open the other window flaps. Soon the air in the coach was a little cooler and you could feel it come in through the open windows.

The stage driver's voice came in through the open windows. "Boulder Point in about one hour."

Harry knew this is where they would be spending the night.

Boulder Point was a fairly large town with five saloons, dance halls, gambling establishments, a telegraph office and several rooming houses, each having a dining area.

As in the past, out of respect for local law enforcement, Harry located the sheriff's office where he would introduce himself. As Harry stepped into the sheriff's office, he was surprised to see a young boy of twelve or so sitting behind the sheriff's desk.

"Well. Don't tell me you're the sheriff here, son," Harry asked, walking up to the desk and extending my hand. "I'm US Marshall Harry Finch."

"I'm Robbie Taylor," he said standing up and grasping Harry's hand in a manly hand shake.

Smiling Robbie said, "No, I'm not the sheriff, but I'm gonna be someday." As he said that, his smile got larger and he continued, "Who knows, maybe a US Marshal even."

Looking at this young boy standing there, Harry could see him as the sheriff or even a US Marshal.

"Well son, you'll make a good one, whichever you choose. Now tell me, where might I fine the sheriff?"

"Sheriff Carter had to go out of town on business," Harry was told. "He had me stay here to deliver this telegram he received from the sheriff of Cinnamon Hollow if you stopped in, which he said you might do once you got to town."

With that, Robbie handed a piece of paper to Harry which was folded in half. As he took the paper from Robbie, he unfolded it, reading the words to himself.

"Another killing. Same as the others. Waiting for your arrival tomorrow."

"Did you read this telegram?" he asked Robbie. "Remember, you want to become a sheriff or even a US Marshal someday so you must always speak the truth."

"No sir," came Robbie's reply. "Only the telegraph operator and Sheriff Carter have read it."

"Well, if you did read it, you must keep this information to yourself, understand?"

"I understand Marshal, but I didn't read it. I was only told to give it to you and no one else."

"Do you live here in town?" he asked the boy.

"Yes, I do. My dad owns the livery stable and we live above it," he continued. Ma passed away this past spring after falling from a horse."

"I'm sorry to hear that," he told him. Reaching into his pocket, he took out a coin and handed it to him. "Go get yourself a soda pop."

"Thanks, Marshal, but you don't have to give me anything."

"I want to. Take it as appreciation. By the way, did the sheriff say when he would return?"

"No he didn't, but he stays here in the jail house and keeps his horse at the livery so I will tell him you're here when he returns."

"Thanks Robbie," Harry said, once again extending his hand.

With that handshake, he left the sheriff's office and walked across the street to the first rooming house he came to. Harry saw that the O'Connor's and Miss DuPont were checked in here also.

The smell of food made him hungry, but he wanted to go to his room to wash some of the trail dust from his face, change his shirt, and ponder that telegram he had received.

"Another killing. Same as the others."

Chapter 2

There wasn't much sense in trying to figure anything out without knowing all of the facts, so after washing off an inch of dust and changing his shirt, Harry made his way to the dining room where he saw Miss DuPont sitting at a table with a middle aged gentleman. Upon questioning his server, Harry learned he was a lawyer in town.

Harry couldn't remember the last time he had enjoyed such a meal as he just had. The steak was thick, juicy, and cooked to perfection. The potatoes were heaped high with a capping of dark, rich gravy. Coffee was fresh, hot, and strong, and the cobbler was served hot.

Miss DuPont was still at her table with her lawyer friend when Harry left.

Walking around town, he saw a couple of girls who were obviously prostitutes and his mind returned to the killing of, what is now, four of Cinnamon Hollow's Painted Ladies.

Harry didn't sleep well thinking of the new body that was discovered just last night and wouldn't until he could get some questions answered. That wouldn't be until tomorrow when he reached Cinnamon Hollow. He expected to see Miss DuPont the next morning at breakfast, but she never showed up. So he ate a hearty breakfast of flapjacks, fried potatoes and again, fresh, hot, strong coffee.

The stage was hitched and ready to go when Harry reached the station and so was Miss DuPont, who gave him a warm smile and a pleasant good-morning.

"Miss DuPont," Harry replied, tipping his hat in response. "Hope your evening was pleasant."

"It was, thank you, and yours?"

"It was okay. When I'm away on an assignment, I tend to keep to myself. Besides, I'm newly married, so the wild night life has been put away."

Looking around the station, Harry didn't see the O'Connor's.

"Benjamin and Catherine are going to miss the stage, if they don't show up here in the next few minutes," Harry said. Suddenly, for some reason he had a bad feeling concerning Catherine.

About that time, Harry saw a very distraught looking Benjamin walking toward him.

"Mr. O'Connor," Harry said, walking toward him. "What's wrong, and where is Mrs. O'Connor?"

"My Catherine is dead," he said, his voice low and shaky.

"What do you mean she's dead?" Harry questioned. "How can that be?"

"When we went to bed last evening, Catherine told me she wasn't feeling well. I got her a glass of water of which she took a couple of sips."

Here, Harry heard his voice start to crack.

"This morning when I woke up, she wasn't breathing and her body was cold. She is with the town doctor now."

At the mention of Catherine's death, Harry heard the sharp intake of breath from Miss DuPont.

"Harry," she whispered, placing her hand on his arm.

Harry wanted to stay but couldn't, not since there was another killing in Cinnamon Hollow.

"If you will locate Rosy O'Neil for me and tell her I will be a couple of days late, then I will stay here with Mr. O'Connor till all arrangements can be made for Mrs. O'Connor."

"I will," he told her and before any more could be said the stage driver yelled into the air, "All aboard!"

* * * * *

When the fourth nude, mutilated body of one of Cinnamon Hollow's Painted Ladies was discovered, Sheriff Tom Evers knew he had made the right decision in contacting the Department of US Marshals.

The newest body to be discovered was one of Sing Lin's girls. This meant that all three madams had girls killed and still no one had any information on who it might be.

The killer had once again worked under cover of darkness, dumping the body where it would be found, at least that is the one thing Sheriff Evers was pretty sure of.

His reasoning for thinking that was, there was very little blood at the scene. Also, with the mutilation done to the body, there had to be some screaming involved and no one had heard anything, and thirdly, there were never any clothes found at the scenes of any of the killings.

As much as Sing Lin wanted the girl's body, Sheriff Evers was holding it at Doc Park's office until Marshal Finch arrived and could take a look and see what his thoughts were. This latest killing would have some of the town's people worried, but most would see that whoever the killer was, he was targeting the town's prostitutes and not them.

Sitting in his office, sipping his morning coffee, Tom was killing time waiting for the stage and the arrival of US Marshal Harry Finch. He started a folder on the girls who had been killed with as much information as he could, which turned out to be little or nothing other than a name and age.

All the dead worked as Painted Ladies, this being the name given to the town's prostitutes. All of the dead women had been discovered nude and their bodies mutilated by having their breasts cut off and multiple knife wounds throughout their bodies, and what looked to be burn marks from a branding iron in the letter 'W'.

Tom had looked closely at this last girl. She was oriental and appeared to be younger than the others. Her face still wore the look of horror and pain. He would wait until Marshal Finch arrived before talking to Sing Lin, who he figured the girl worked for.

In the past, he hadn't paid too much attention to the town's Painted Ladies. They stayed to themselves in the saloons and dance halls and created no trouble. Now, he made a note to get all of their names, just in case more killings took place. With this fourth one, it appeared more than likely that might happen.

The first two bodies had been found just outside of town, where these last two were in town and quite out in the open, so they would be found quickly.

* * * * *

Tom heard the loud footsteps on the boardwalk in front of his office, before the door opened and in walked Mayor Dwayne McIntire.

Tom and Dewayne had been friends since childhood. They had grown up together and were best friends. Dewayne had been elected mayor five years ago and when Sheriff Wright retired, he asked Tom if he wanted the job.

Tom had always wanted to be a sheriff or a Texas Ranger, so after talking it over with his wife, he sold his livery stable business and took the job. He was already well known and liked by the town's people, so he fit right in.

Only in his third year on the job, he had never experienced anything like what was happening, so he had talked with his friend, the mayor, and decided to ask for help before this got out of hand.

"Mr. Mayor," Tom said, getting up from behind his desk and walking over to his friend with hand extended.

"Morning, Tom," Dewayne said, taking the hand in a firm grip. "Is that a pot of fresh coffee you got there?" he asked, pointing toward the pot belly stove in the corner.

"You know me. Doesn't matter how hot it gets, there's always a fresh pot of coffee brewing."

"Must say, having my morning coffee here, sure smells a lot nicer than when it was in that old horse stable," a remark that put a smile on both their faces.

"That it does," was Tom's reply.

Tom also had a blacksmith shop in his livery stable. He was always up and about early and would have his coffee brewing early in the mornings. Dewayne was an early riser, too. He would be out for his morning walk and would stop by for a cup of coffee and make small talk as to what was going on in their town.

Now, Tom was still up early and still brewing his coffee, accustomed to the heat from his blacksmith shop.

"The Marshal you asked for arrives today. Right?" Dewayne asked, pouring himself a cup of coffee.

As the hot liquid hit the cup, spirals of steam rose from it, sending a smell into the air that invaded the nose buds, waking them up, along with the far away sound of a barking dog and the morning call of a cock rooster, who for some reason had decided to make his home right next door to his office.

"Awwwww," Dewayne moaned at the first sip of the hot liquid. "All the good things about being up and about in the morning. A good friend's voice, a hot coffee, a barking dog, and the morning call of a rooster, who really needs to be in an oven!" A remark that brought a chuckle from them both.

"I see you're already busy getting ready for the Marshal's arrival later today," Dewayne said, offering to refill his friend's cup.

"No, thanks. Been here for a while now and that's the second pot I've made. Any more right now and I'll have to spend the day in the outhouse out back."

There wasn't much more Tom could do, so he offered to walk around town.

"Let's go," Dewayne said, putting his cup down and reaching for the door knob at the same time.

Outside, both stood looking out over the town. Both took in deep breaths and exhaled loudly.

"No better time in the day than right now," exclaimed Dewayne, who had been taking these morning walks for as long as his memories could recall.

"Yes sir. The air is fresh and clear, having the dust settled from it. Basically quiet, free from all the hustle and bustle noises of the day's activities."

"It sure is," Tom agreed, placing his hand on the mayor's shoulder.

Tom, who himself was an early riser, had been noticing his friend and also mayor, was stopping in earlier and earlier in the mornings. This morning, even before the old cock rooster had crowed.

As the two stood there looking over the town with admiration, Tom asked his friend,

"Is there something pressing on your mind this morning, Dewayne?" his voice low and concerned.

"Town's growing, more and more responsibility, and now with these killings," Dewayne's head hung low and pivoted back and forth.

"Listen!" Tom stated. "You do what you do the best. And that is running this town! Leave the sheriffing business up to me. These killings will be handled and then everyone can relax again," here Tom gave the shoulder he had placed his hand on a little shake.

As they walked, they came to the Cinnamon Hollow Feed & Mercantile Store which was just opening up.

Tillie, the town's nickname for the owner, believed in being open early just in case someone needed to purchase something. That someone being Tom, who always had a small paper bag containing some rock candy in his pocket, which he would hand out to the children he might run into throughout the day.

'I guess you might say it was a way of getting them to respect law enforcement,' he would think to himself when asked why he did it.

Tillie stepped out, just as they approached his store.

"Morning, gents," he said to them both.

"Morning, Tillie," came their reply.

"Got some new strawberry flavored rock candy that just arrived, Tom," he mentioned when they had stopped, knowing Tom would come in and spend a few pennies on the hard candy.

"Strawberry flavored, you say? Why, I need to be trying some of that."

Tom's sweet tooth came alive in his mouth at the sight of all the candy jars lined up on the counter top, but the jar that caught his attention was the one that contained the red crystals associated with rock candy.

Tillie reached into the jar and broke off a small piece which he handed to Tom.

Popping the piece of red crystal in his mouth, Tom sort of swished it back and forth, while also sucking on it. Seconds later, as the flavor of wild strawberries reached his taste buds, a big grin lit up his face.

"Wow! You need to be trying a piece of this," he told Dewayne, reaching into the jar and taking out another small piece to hand his friend.

"I'm charging you for that one," Tillie told Tom.

Dewayne had to agree, the candy sure tasted like wild strawberries.

Taking a dime from his pocket, Tom placed it on the counter.

"Give me a dime's worth, Tillie," he said motioning to the coin he had placed on the counter, "and you be sure to keep a good supply of that on hand."

Taking the small brown paper bag that Tillie handed him, Tom put it in his pocket, thanked him then he and Dewayne left the store with Tom happier than when he went in.

Several of the town's people stopped them and asked if it was true that another woman had been killed and if so, was she one of the town's Painted Ladies."

For all those who asked, Tom gave them the same answer.

"A woman had been found and she was with the doctor now being examined, and when I get the doctor's finding I will let you all know."

"I'm sure glad you have that US Marshal coming," Dewayne told him, after being stopped several more times.

Both Dewayne and Tom stopped in the doctor's office to see what he had discovered.

"You were right, Sheriff, whoever killed those other whores, also killed this one," the doctor told them.

Doctor Thurston Parks was a little old man who told things like he saw them. He wasn't a lover of having whores in what he considered to be his town and he made no gripes about his feelings, even refusing to glamorize what they were by calling them Painted Ladies.

"They're whores, plain and simple," he would call them, if asked.

Right up till that very minute, Tom had forgotten that Doc had served time in prison after catching his wife whoring around on him. Even now, years later, Tom picked up animosity in his voice.

'I wonder?' That being a question that entered Tom's thinking, and he made a mental note to tell the marshal about him.

"I'll be back in a little while," Tom told the Doc. "We can then discuss your findings on all the women you've examined," Tom told him, preferring that the marshal was also present.

"Women are too good of a name to call them. Fact is, they're whores. Flat out, plain and simple."

"Regardless of your feeling, Doc, these women didn't deserve to die like this."

Making eye contact with Dewayne, Tom gave him a slight nod indicating it was time to leave.

"I don't understand, Tom. Why didn't you question him more about the body?" Dewayne asked, curious to hear Tom's answer.

"I will, but felt that the US Marshal should be present. That way he doesn't hear it second hand from me."

"Old Doc sure doesn't pull any punches when it comes to speaking out how he feels about Painted Ladies. Why heck, I can't even use the word he uses," Dewayne said.

"That's another story I'll wait to tell once the marshal arrives," said Tom.

The eleven-fifty stage was right on time and Tom was there to meet it, anxious to meet this US Marshal Finch.

There was only one passenger to get off the stage, and he was nothing like what Tom had visualized in his mind as to what Marshal Finch would look like.

The man getting off the stage was in his mid to late twenties and stood over six feet tall with a full head of hair and a clean shaven face, unlike the middle-aged, short, stocky, balding figure, sporting big, bushy eye brows and a bushy mustache he had visualized.

Harry smiled as he saw the man walking towards him. The badge pinned to his vest told him that this must be Sheriff Tom Evers.

Tom was still a couple footsteps away when he asked, "Are you Marshal Finch. Harry Finch?"

"Yes I am," Harry assured him. "And you must be Sheriff Tom Evers," he said in return.

"Yes I am, but let's get rid of the formalities, you can call me Tom."

"Alright, Tom. You call me Harry." he told him, hand outstretched which he took in a firm grip.

"No one else on the stage?" Tom asked.

"There was. I'll tell you all about it. But first, I want to get checked in, wash, change my shirt, get a cup of coffee and hear all about these killings."

Picking up his bag, Tom pointed in the direction of the Cinnamon Hollow Rooming House and Dance Emporium.

Chapter 3

Once Harry washed and changed his shirt, he met Tom and headed for his office where he told Harry there was a pot of the best coffee in town. He wasn't kidding. The hot, strong liquid awakened Harry's taste buds.

"Let me say thank you, Harry, for getting out here so quickly. I felt I was in way over my head on this one, and now with this fourth killing, I know I made the right decision in contacting the bureau to get someone out here."

"Well, Tom, I haven't had any experience in this sort of thing either, so it will be learn as we go for us both," Harry told him. "So, let's get down to it. What do you have so far?"

"Not much. But before we start, I told the mayor I would bring you around to his office. He is staying there till we arrive."

"Well then, let's get on to the mayor's office," Harry told him. "We need to get started on this case as soon as possible."

Before leaving his office, Harry removed his badge and put it in his vest pocket.

"No need to play our hand yet," he told Tom. "We don't know who this killer is, or for that matter, if he is still here. So let's not expose who I am right now."

Tom agreed so they left his office and walked the short distance to the mayor's office.

The mayor was seated at his desk when they entered, but looking up and seeing who they were, brought him to his feet and he walked out from behind his desk to greet them.

"Mayor, this is US Marshal Harry Finch. Better known as just Harry," was Tom's way of introducing him.

"Well Harry, I'm Dewayne Macintyre the Mayor of Cinnamon Hollow. Welcome," he said grasping Harry's hand and shaking it.

"Folks around either call me Mayor or Dewayne, unless I'm doing official business."

"I like the sound of 'Mayor,' but call me Harry. I don't want anyone to know my official title just yet. People tend to talk more to a stranger than a Marshal, especially in this circumstance."

"Okay. Harry it will be," he said. "Have you had anything to eat? Are you checked into the rooming house yet?"

"I'm checked into the Cinnamon Hollow Rooming House but I haven't had anything to eat yet," he told him. "There are some things I want to do before food."

"They do up a fine steak where you're staying," Dwayne advised. "And Tom makes the best coffee in town."

"I've had his coffee and agree. It is mighty fine."

It was time to end the chit chat and get down to business.

"Tom," Harry said. "Let's go back to your office, seeing as I will be using that as my center of operation. We can stop by my room, so I can get a few things on the way."

Extending his hand again, Harry said, "Nice to meet you Mayor."

"Same here, Harry."

Handshake done, Harry turned to Tom, nodded, and he opened the office door. They walked out onto the street and made their way to Harry's room, after being stopped several times on the way and asked about the dead woman.

Once back in Tom's office, he offered Harry his desk, which he refused, but Tom insisted. Taking his chair, Harry placed his pad on the desk, took out his pencil and they started.

"Tell me what is known about the killings so far," starting to list what Tom told Harry.

"The first girl found worked for Rosy O'Neil, known as Big Rear Rosy, for obvious reasons. Her name was Priscilla Wilcox. As a dancer, bar girl and a Painted Lady she was known as Cilla."

Waiting for Harry to write that down, Tom stoked the fire and checked the coffee pot.

"Next," Harry said, waiting a few minutes for him to get a fresh pot boiling.

"Second worked for Millie. She runs a bordello and her girls are strictly Painted Ladies. I don't have her last name, but she is known as Magnificent Millie."

"What is she known as Magnificent for?" Harry asked, wondering why all women who work as prostitutes he hears about always sport some sort of nickname.

"I guess because of her charm and the fact all her girls, plus herself are beautiful."

"How's that coffee coming?" Harry asked, smelling its rich aroma.

"A few more minutes," he told Harry.

Seeing Harry had finished writing, he continued.

"Third girl was another one of Rosy's. Her name was Connie Hunter, and she went by Kitty."

Coffee done, Tom poured two cups and handed him one. It smelled delicious. A good cup of coffee has a different aroma to it and over time, Harry had learned that. Now he could tell what to expect from just the smell, and this was delicious smelling,

"The last girl found worked just outside of town for Sing Lin. She was Chinese and her name was Mae Day."

"Are these the only three Madam's in Cinnamon Hollow?", Harry asked, "Or are there more?"

"Those are the only three, Harry, and I haven't really talked to them much because I was waiting for you to get here. I did tell them I had sent for a US Marshal and for their girls to be careful and not to take any chances, if approached by someone who seems strange. Of course, they wanted to know what I meant by strange."

"How many girls work for each one of these Madams I have listed here?"

Stopping him from answering, Harry told him to go and bring one of them to the office.

"Don't take no for an answer," Harry told him. "I need to speak with each one as soon as possible."

"Shouldn't be long, Harry. Rosy is only up the street and it is still light out, so not much is happening in any of the saloons right now."

Harry watched as he left, wondering what was happening here in Cinnamon Hollow and at the same time hoping no other killing would take place tonight.

Tom wasn't aware of the set of eyes that followed him from the shadows of the alley. Ten minutes later, as he returned with Rosy, he was still unaware of the set of eyes that followed him, as the two entered his office.

Tom introduced Rosy O'Neil to Harry, then offered her a coffee and a chair, of which she took the chair and refused the coffee.

Harry started out asking some standard questions to get some of her history before asking about the girls who worked for her that had been mutilated and killed.

"My girls are known as Rosy's Roses," she told him. "There have been two of my Roses killed. They were, Priscilla Wilcox known as Cilla, and Connie Hunter, known as Kitty. Both were in their late twenties and were dancers, bar girls, singers, and Painted Ladies," she answered, concerning the two dead women. "Both were well liked by all, and had been with me for about four years," she continued.

"Had either one of these two mentioned anyone in particular they were scared about, or who might have wanted to do them harm?"

"No, Marshal. None of my girls have," she answered after taking a minute or so to think back. "As I said, all my girls are well liked by everyone."

"How many girls do you have working for you right now?" Harry asked.

"I have four right now," she answered. "I have another coming who was supposed to have arrived on the stage today, but she never did."

"Is her name Della DuPont?" Harry asked, getting a surprised look from Rosy at the mention of her name.

"Why, how could you have possibly known that?" she questioned. "Do you know her?"

"Not really. She was on the stage I was on. One of the three passengers died and she stayed in Boulder Point to help her husband, who didn't know anyone, settle matters up. She should be coming in on the stage tomorrow," Harry told her. "She wanted me to give you that message."

"She is okay though?"

You could see a look of relief on her face once Harry told her about Della.

"I had to identify the dead girls, Marshal. Who could have done such a horrible, horrible thing to another human being?"

"That's what Marshal Finch is here to find out," Tom told her.

"You know me, Tom. None of my girls have ever caused any trouble in town in all the years we have been here."

"I want to thank you for all the information you were able to give me," Harry told her. "If I have any more questions I'll send word by Tom. Will that be okay?" Harry inquired. "Better yet. I will probably want to speak at some time ahead to all of your girls. You won't object to that will you?"

"Of course not, Marshal. Just let me know what I can help with and I will be more than happy to help out."

Harry shook Rosy's hand and Tom walked her out. They had been a little over an hour and Harry decided that was all he was going to do today, as far as speaking to the other Madam's.

The eyes that had watched from the shadows earlier, were no longer there. The only telltale sign of someone being there were three cigarette butts that had been ground out in the dirt.

Moments later, Tom returned. Walking over and checking the coffee pot, Tom motioned to Harry, if he wanted a refill.

"No thanks, Tom. What I would like is to get something to eat, then return here and plan out tomorrow. Is that good with you, or do you need to be underway?" Harry was hoping Tom would stay and join him, and was happy when Tom told Harry he was available anytime day or night, until this was solved.

"Let's go get something to eat then, shall we?" Harry asked.

"You bet. What's your stomach in the mood for?" was Tom's only question.

"You choose," Harry told him. "I eat just about anything."

The sign painted on the window said, "Sally's. Home cooked meals."

"Here we go," Tom said, opening the door and letting Harry step through.

Instantly, Harry's senses were invaded by an array of odors. Fried chicken, ham, bacon, coffee, and cigarette smoke.

"Can't get a bad meal in here," Tom told Harry, sitting at a corner table.

Harry noticed there was a blackboard on the wall and there was their menu written on it in chalk.

"I'm having the ham steak with home fried potatoes," he told me. "My favorite."

"I like your choice. I'll have the same."

A smile is all their waitress offered and Tom told Harry she couldn't speak. None of the girls could speak, Harry noticed. When Harry mentioned this to Tom, he gave him a smile and told Harry why.

"Sally wanted to be able to serve as many meals as she could, and didn't want her girls spending time chit chatting with the patrons. So she started hiring those that couldn't speak. The townspeople supported her because they thought she was giving those who were handicapped a chance to make a living, so her decision became two fold."

Tom had been right. The ham steak and fried potatoes were very good. The meal had also come with coffee and a biscuit. The apple pie was extra and was a big enough slice that it could have fed them both.

Getting up to leave, Tom said to Sally, "Put that on my tab, will ya Sally," Tom and the mayor had decided that Cinnamon Hollow would take care of a few of the marshal's meals, while he was here.

"I appreciate the town wanting to cover my meals, Tom, but I get my meals and room paid for by the bureau, when I am on an assignment."

"The Mayor and I wasn't sure how that went, so we set it up with Sally to run a tab and the town would pay it," Tom thought for a moment and told Harry, "Why don't the times you eat at Sally's, you put that meal on the tab. I won't always be eating all meals with you as I have other business to do in town."

Checking his watch and seeing it was getting later than Harry expected, he told Tom it was time to call it quits for the day and he would meet him at his office in the morning.

"I want to talk with the other two madams as early as possible, then I want to speak with the doctor and see this last victim."

"That reminds me Harry, make sure you ask me to tell you about Doctor Parks in the morning."

As they said their good nights out in front of Sally's, neither one heard the woman's scream coming from the root cellar located on Willard Wright's abandoned place.

Chapter 4

The root cellar had been dug deeper into the ground, making it a room of about ten by ten which was more than large enough to carry on the ghastly things going on inside. The depth into the earth and a big heavy door guaranteed that no sound could be heard on the outside.

This is why the screams echoing off the inside walls of the root cellar went unheard as the hot branding iron sizzled the soft flesh sending the nauseous odor of burnt flesh into the air, as it left the sign of a 'W' on the woman's stomach. This was the part he enjoyed the most, watching their form twist and turn trying to get away from the white hot branding iron, their faces marred in pain. He used to gag them, but now he let them scream, this adding to his sadistic enjoyment.

It had been two nights since his last victim.

An evil smile came over his face, as he remembered the screams that came from the mouth of the little Chinese whore when he branded the bottom of her feet, then passing out from the pain, only to be revived by a bucket of cold water.

He had made a vow to rid the town of all the whores, or die trying. He had watched from the alley at the stranger who had come to town and was united with Sheriff Tom. So he summed up that he was some kind of lawman, which is why he had decided to give him a welcoming present of this young whore.

He originally was going to grab Dixie who worked for Millie, but when the little Chinese whore walked right by him in the alley, he couldn't resist the ease that was presented to him, so he grabbed her instead.

And now, he was having so much fun with this little Chinese whore, he was saddened some in knowing he would kill her shortly and dump her body to be found in the morning. Something had snapped in his head with the first killing and now he was like a mad man who couldn't get enough.

Another blood curdling scream filled the room as the branding iron sizzled her flesh lower down on her stomach, leaving another ghastly wound in the shape of a 'W'. He had already thrown some cold water on her, denying her the comfort of passing out.

"Where would you like the next one to be," he bent down and whispered in her left ear.

"Here?" he asked, stabbing his finger into her left side just below her heaving breast. Just the stabbing with his finger caused her to scream.

"Or here," he asked again, poking his finger into her left thigh.

While she was thinking about those two areas, he put the branding iron against the inside of her right thigh and held it there, burning its way through flesh and muscle all the way to the bone. There wasn't enough water in the bucket to revive her this time and the odor of burned flesh even got to him, so he laid down the branding iron, opened the cellar door, and stepped out into the night's fresh air.

It was almost like daytime, once he got outside. The full moon had risen into the night sky and its bright silvery color blanketed the landscape. The night was quiet. A testimony to how well his dungeon of torture was at insulating sound from the outside world.

These intervals between tortures he enjoyed almost as much as when he was in the middle of the act itself. He could reflect on the impact the different forms of torture were having on his victims.

This first break in torture always ended the same. Standing, he would unsnap his pants so that he could reach around inside them to run his hand over his right rear cheek to feel the 'W' that was his own branding.

He could recall that day as though it were yesterday.

He grew up on a small mid-western cattle ranch along with two sisters. Once old enough to help out around the ranch, they were all given chores they had to do, and were punished severely if they didn't.

As he grew older, he noticed the punishment took on a different temperament. Instead of a couple of belt lashings across the backside, it might be drawn out over several minutes, where both his mom and dad would hand out the lashings.

If you dropped or spilt something, you could expect mom to place one, two, or even three of your fingers on the hot stoves surface, holding them there as you kicked and screamed.

You did your best to stay away from either if they had a cigarette, because you could expect them to burn you with it, and if they couldn't manage at least one burn during the day, expect to be wakened from a sound sleep by your scream as one would be extinguished on the bottom of a foot, hand, or wherever they felt like it.

When we were younger, they would take us after we fell asleep down to the creek, remove our sleeping clothes, and throw us naked into that cold creek. Even now, years and years later, this thought brought shivers to his body.

Thinking back now on all that pain, none could compare with the anguish and blood curdling screams from both his sisters and himself as the day they were all branded. The branding of the new calves done, their mom and dad had decided that their children needed branding also.

Standing there now, running his hand over his brand mark, he recalled the many times they would all be swimming in the creek naked, the branding mark on both his mom and dad.

He watched as both his sisters were bent over their father's knee and their bottoms were laid bare and their mom, yielding the white hot branding iron, laid it firmly against one cheek. Instantly, legs flared out and screams echoed off the distant mountains. Afterward, a trip to the creek helped reduce the pain.

As these memories flooded back, he had second thoughts of waiting to kill this one until after he found out who the stranger was with the sheriff. If it turned out to be a US Marshal, then he would need to be more careful and there was no need to play cat and mouse with him yet.

Entering the root cellar once again, he approached the squirming girl bound to the table and bent down and whispered into her ear.

"Well, little lady. You get to live another day."

* * *

Outside of the saloons and dance halls, Cinnamon Hollow was asleep under a silvery blanket cast over it by the full moon.

Harry loved nights like this when he could see almost as plain as in the daylight, but without all the noises associated with the day.

If it wasn't for the ruckus the saloons and dance halls created, this would be an almost perfect night. Harry thought as he left the sheriff's office and headed to his room.

Suddenly, all the hairs on his neck jumped to attention. This being a sixth sense he had developed over time as a warning of impending danger. At the same time, he thought he saw a movement in the alley across the street.

Placing his hand over his sidearm, Harry crossed the street and entered the alley. As he did, the hairs on his neck which had been at attention, now relaxed. Even so, Harry slowly walked the alley checking all the shadows, but found no one.

Blinking his eyes to accustom them to the shadows, Harry realized for the first time that day, how tired he had become. So he left the alley and walked to his room, where he simply plopped himself down on the bed. Moments later, the sounds of deep sleep could be heard coming from inside his room.

The loud knocking on his door, startled Harry awake.

"Harry, Harry. Are you in there?" Harry recognized the voice as Tom's.

"Yes, yes! Just a minute, Tom," Harry replied. Checking his watch, Harry saw it was after eight o'clock.

Harry opened the door and was greeted by Tom and the clerk, who Tom dismissed as soon as he made sure Harry was okay.

"Boy! I haven't had a sleep like that in ages," he told Tom who had entered his room.

"Thanks for coming to get me. Now, do you have a pot of coffee on?"

"Always. I've been waiting for you and when it started to get late, I grew worried about you."

"I'm okay. Why don't you give me a few minutes to wash and change, then I'll meet you in your office and have a coffee. Afterwards, I want to go look at something before we eat."

"Sounds good, Harry," Tom replied, walking from the room.

Ten minutes later, Harry had a cup of hot coffee half drunk, sipping the hot, black liquid in silence.

"Didn't quite know what to expect when you didn't show up first thing this morning, Harry. Hope you don't mind me calling on ya this morning, but I had looked for you in the dining room and no one had seen you.

"No, I don't mind," Harry told him finishing my cup and pouring another.

"Sure is mighty tasty coffee, Tom. Who taught you to make it?"

"An old man from Tennessee who was passing through on his way west to the gold fields. Wasn't much he didn't know."

"Ready for that walk, Tom?" Harry asked, draining his coffee cup, wondering what he would find, if anything, in the alley.

As we made our way to the alley, Harry told Tom about seeing someone there last night.

"Just what do you expect to find there, Harry?" asked Tom as they made their way there.

"Any signs that someone had been there for a while. Cigarette butts, empty whiskey bottle, even where someone might have taken a leak."

The only things in the alley were some wooden crates and four wooden barrels, of which, two were stacked on top of each other which would offer a person a good hiding place from where he could observe anyone coming and going from the sheriff's office or the Cinnamon Hollow Saloon and Rooming House. Other than some footprints in the loose dirt, there were no signs that anyone had been looking out from there.

"I don't see anything here, Harry! Are you sure you saw someone?"

"I'm sure of it," Harry told him. "I also have this sixth sense where the hair on my neck stiffens as a warning. Over the years, I've nurtured this and today it acts as another set of eyes and ears. Last night, not only was I sure I saw the shadow of someone in this alley, the hairs on my neck were stiff."

They walked around for several more minutes, then Harry told Tom to go bring in another one of the Madams, so they could question her.

Returning to the office Harry found the mayor outside the door talking to a gentleman sporting an apron which, by all the ink stains told Harry he must be the local editor or newspaper man of some sort.

As always, his thought were correct.

"Good morning, Mayor," Harry said as he approached them. "Nice morning to be out and about."

"That it is, Harry, though it is getting along into the day."

"Yes it is," Harry said, motioning for the mayor to step into the office. "What brings you around?"

"I wanted to introduce you to the owner and editor of the Cinnamon Hollow Gazette, Carl Murdock. Carl, this is US Marshal Harry Finch. Harry's working with Tom on these killings."

Harry took the extended hand and gave it a shake. "Mr. Murdock," was all he offered for now.

Harry had met quite a number of newspaper men over the year, and had found out, with anything that walks, talks, and breathes, you have your good ones and bad ones. Until he discovered which you were, he was going to keep any conversation low keyed.

"Pleased to meet you, Marshal. Tom had asked me to hold off printing anything concerning the killings we've had of the local Painted Ladies until after you arrived. I agreed to not print anything, but the townspeople have been wanting to know what's going on. Many are concerned, as right they should be."

"Well, Mr. Murdock, as you know."

"Call me Carl," he interrupted.

"Okay Carl. As I started to say, I just got here and Tom and I have just started to question some of the people who might be able to answer those questions that will get us to the bottom of these killings. In the meantime, I would ask you to continue not to print anything unless it comes from me or Tom. I'll give you a short clip to print that should put most folk at ease."

Judging by the look on Carl's face, Harry could tell he was going to want more. So thinking for a minute, Harry made him an offer that Harry was pretty sure Carl couldn't turn down.

"I'll tell you what I can do, if you hold off printing this story right now. I'll let you hang with us and you can have firsthand knowledge of what we find out as this investigation goes on, that way, you can keep notes and when it is solved, you will have the makings of a book, rather than just a newspaper story."

As Harry guessed, Carl's eyes lit up and he immediately agreed. "Okay, then. Go get your notepad and join us back at Tom's office and we will begin putting down what we have learned so far on a timeline.

"Taking a big chance there on Carl, aren't you Harry?" asked the mayor when he had disappeared.

"I don't think so, Mayor. Carl is just wanting to do his story to keep the people informed as to these killings which have been going on."

Tom had coffee boiling, when Carl returned. An extra chair had been pulled up in front of the desk for Carl as well as a coffee cup.

"Coffee is just about done, Harry," Tom told him, at the same time motioning for Carl to take a seat.

"Great, Tom," replied Harry. "Let's get started on what we know so far."

And with that, they went over all that was known up till now.

Chapter 5

After having their first cup of coffee the next morning, Harry had Tom go and locate Sing Lin and tell her she had to come to the office to answer some questions. Sing Lin was another Madam in town, but unlike the other two, she ran her business outside of town and tents were what they worked out of.

It was a pretty good set-up with a large tent that held a makeshift bar which was a long plank acting as a bar top laid across two barrels. Some empty powder kegs acted as stools.

There were three tables where the clients could also sit and be waited on by her girls who displayed themselves and would sit on laps and show off some skin hoping to be chosen. Several smaller tents acted as individual rooms where the girls took their customers.

Tom had been known to visit Sing Lin's establishment having been taken in by one of her girls. A young, sweet, girl by the name of Lui Chang. Tom's heart had his eyes closed as to what she did for work. He didn't care. It didn't matter to him if she cost him money, because here was a girl who paid attention to him.

Tom felt she had those same feelings for him and was getting ready to ask her if she would be his wife and give up what she was doing. Tom had decided that morning he would talk to Harry about her and see what he had to say and what advice he could give. Although Tom knew most of the townspeople, he didn't have a close friend he could confide in, and since meeting Harry, he felt a bond he hadn't felt with any man before.

Although it was still early in the morning, Tom found Sing Lin was up and cleaning the main tent. He heard laughter coming from the river that flowed just behind their tents and figured the girls must be taking baths and such. He longed to go and see if Lui Chang was one of them.

Tom didn't know much about Sing Lin and her girls that occupied the tents, other than what they did. They kept to themselves and Sing Lin was the only one he had ever seen in town, whenever they needed supplies. Always on foot, she would make several trips to gather her supplies.

It was only out of curiosity that Tom had visited her establishment. There he met Lui Chang and fell in love with her at first sight. Now he visited there two, maybe three times a week to see Lui Chang. Most of the time his visits were done mid-day, as not to run into anyone who might know him. No one was ever there at this timee

Tom knew that during the day, the two brothels were pretty quiet. Although there always seemed to be some customers there, it wasn't until after suppertime they got busy.

Tom was surprised that Sing Lin spoke such good English and was happy to go with him to town. She disappeared for a few minutes then returned and told him let's go.

Tom rode and Sing Lin walked the short distance into town, neither saying a word to each other, but Tom noticed her facial expression was one of pain and there was a limp to her step.

Sing Lin waited as Tom hitched his horse, then they entered the sheriff's office together. Both Carl and Harry stood when she entered. Pointing to an empty chair, Harry offered her a cup of coffee at the same time.

"Tea?" she asked.

"Tom, will you run over to the Cinnamon Hollow and bring back some tea for Sing Lin? I'll wait until you return before asking her any questions."

"Sure, Harry," Tom left and returned several minutes later with a steaming cup of tea, for which Sing Lin thanked him.

"I'm US Marshal Harry Finch," he began. "You probably know the newspaper editor Carl Murdock and Tom, the sheriff."

Sing Lin nodded her head.

"You know, Sing Lin, we found a dead Chinese girl that we need to know about. She is at the undertakers and we would like you to go and identify her."

"I don't have to Marshal, I already know who she is," Sing Lin told him in perfect English. "Her name was Wong Lee, but she went by Golden Honey."

"When did you see her last?" he questioned. "I have been told your girls don't come into town."

"They don't usually, but I fell a while back and I have had to send them into town for supplies. That's what Wong Lee was doing in town, picking up supplies."

"So she wasn't in town working?" Harry asked.

"None of my girls work in town," she told Harry. "I don't allow them to. They only come to town when I can't. And now, I have another girl who didn't return."

"What!" it was Tom who spoke out. "You have another girl missing? Who is she?"

Tom was on his feet, heart pounding in his chest hearing her words. Thoughts were racing through his brain and a quick, silent prayer formed on his lips.

Dear GOD. Please don't let it be Lui Chang.

Tom's heart stopped beating when he heard Sing Lin say, "Lui Chang."

"What! You said Lui Chang?" Tom couldn't believe what he was hearing, but he knew what he heard. His Lui Chang was missing.

"Why didn't you come and let the sheriff know?" Harry asked.

"If Lui Chang has been abducted, she will be the fifth girl in a short period of time. All the working girls, not just mine, are getting scared to take on customers. You know what that does for business? Already, my girls don't want to be alone with a customer. So we don't say much to draw any more attention to what is happening here, but it is hard not to be scared when you hear what is done to the girls."

"How do you know what is done to them?" Tom wanted to know.

"We all have some of the same customers who pass on information," she told him. "Plus I go into town every third day or so and I get all the news that I don't otherwise get."

Taking a moment to sip her tea, she continued.

"Now with Lui Chang not coming back from town, I'm worried that she has also fallen prey to whoever is killing all of our girls."

"Have any of your girls said anything about a customer they might have had that showed and kind of hatred to them. Hit them, or was extremely rough?" Harry asked.

"No, Marshal," she told him. "My girls might be younger than most, but they've all been told not to let anyone beat-up on them, so I would have heard if there was anyone like that."

Harry took notes as to what Sing Lin was telling him. He also picked up a difference in Tom's voice at the mention of Lui Chang's name and made a note to ask him about that, but still had some questions for Sing Lin.

"Tell me what you've heard about the killings," Harry asked her, wanting to know exactly what she had heard.

"I'll try, but what I have heard is horrible to speak about," she said and then started to tell what she had heard.

"I heard they had been beat-up and tortured. They had rope burns on their ankles and wrist meaning they were tied up. Their bodies were covered in cigarette burns and had been branded several times with the letter 'W'."

Taking a moment to get her composure, she continued.

"They all had their breast cut off and also their tongues."

Sing Lin actually started to shake at the mention of these last two things, so Harry told her thanks and she could go, but to please talk to her girls and to let either of them know if any of her girls hear anything.

"Thank you Sing Lin for all your help. I'll let you know if Lui Chang shows up or if we get any news concerning her," then Harry asked, "Do you want the body of Golden Honey or do you want us to bury her?"

"Please Marshal, bring her out. We will take care of her."

With that, Sing Lin thanked Tom for the tea and quietly walked from the office. It was obvious to Harry that both Tom and Carl were moved by what they had just heard.

"I've heard from Tom concerning the bodies and what had been done to them, but sitting here and hearing it told by a woman was very troubling," Carl said, breaking the few moments of silence after Sing Lin had left.

"And now, as we gather here, there might be another girl out there undergoing the torture we were just told about," the voice of Carl remarked. Cracking at the end as he stood there shaking his head.

"I'll be right back," Tom said, setting his coffee cup down and walking out.

"Well Carl," Harry finally said, "I told you this was going to be a big story and as you have just heard, it seems just that."

Tom passed several of the townspeople who wished him a good morning and were surprised when he didn't even acknowledge them, but walked on by with a blank look on his face. Tom was deep in thought as he walked, recalling what Sing Lin knew about the girls that were found killed and his own examination of their bodies, and now, his Lui Chang might be the next victim was more than he could comprehend at this time.

"Oh, shhhhhh!" he said out loud when he stepped off the end of the boardwalk and ended up in the street on his butt in a cloud of dust. Instantly, Tom felt the pressure of a helping hand on his arm.

"Let me help you up there, Tom," he heard the voice of Harry say, as he was being lifted up at the same time by Harry's strong arm.

Once on his feet, Harry made the attempt of brushing him off while asking, "are you okay?"

"I'm okay, Harry," he said then changed his tone, too. "No I'm not okay, Harry. It's Lui Chang, the missing girl. We have been seeing each other, and now?"

"Let's go back to the office, Tom. No need to stand here in the middle of the street."

Carl was still in the office, when Tom and Harry returned. As a matter of fact, he had put on a fresh pot of coffee and was going over his notes.

"Fresh coffee in the pot," he said, when they walked in. But before either could pour a cup, the door opened and in walked a stunning looking woman of about thirty-five.

I noticed at quick glance she was expensively dressed in clothes that said, 'Look at me!' She was no ordinary woman and I instantly made her out to be the other Madam in town.

"Harry, I'd like you to meet Miss Millie Cartwright, she is the other Madam in town. I knew you wanted to speak with her, so I sent for her."

Seeing Harry's surprised look, Carl continued.

"I didn't know she would get here so quickly."

"That's alright," Harry told him, before extending his hand toward her in introduction.

"Miss Cartwright, I'm US Marshal Harry Finch. Better known as just plain Harry."

"Well. Just plain Harry," she said, "Folks know me as Magnificent Millie. I own Millie's, one of the brothels in town. You can call me just plain Millie." A remark that brought laughs from everyone.

"Well Millie, I suppose you know that Tom had contacted my main office concerning the killing of some of the town's Painted Ladies. I know one of those dead girls worked for you."

"One of them did. Her name was Kellie Horn. She was a beautiful girl who worked for me these past two years."

"Did she ever complain of someone being overly rough or showed any kind of meanness to her or the other girls?"

Harry was trying to find out if anyone had experienced a bad time with any of their customers. With the brutality of the killings, whoever it was had to show some kind of hatred toward them when dealing with their services, unless whoever it was didn't use their services.

"Tell me some about Kellie. Did she see anyone special when not working?"

"No she didn't, Harry. I have told my girls not to get attached to anyone, if they wanted to work for me. A girl in love doesn't give her all with her customers and besides that, I don't need some boyfriend busting up a customer or worse, out of jealousy," Millie told him.

"Kellie could do it all. Dance, sing, she was beautiful, not only on the outside, but on the inside to. All the other girls liked Kellie. They were always borrowing something from her, but she didn't mind, she liked them to."

"Kellie was the second girl that was killed. Since her death, how have your other girls been?" Harry asked.

"They have always been careful of who they went with, plus my girls are somewhat more expensive than any of the others, so they draw a different clientele," she continued. "Also, my girls only work here. They don't leave and go to someone's room, only their own."

"Do they have customers who stay overnight?" Tom asked, in between Harry's questioning of Millie.

"No they don't. That's not allowed either," she told him and then explained why they didn't.

"Some of the customers who visit my girls are married men. I don't need one of their wives barging in, in the wee hours of the morning looking for their husband, so, overnighters are not allowed, and Tony makes sure that rule is followed," she went on to say.

"Who is Tony?" Harry asked, at the mention of his name.

"Tony is my piano player and overseer of my girls," Millie answered. "He checks up on each one when the night is over to make sure they are alone in their rooms. I have never had any problems with any of my girls until Kellie disappeared and later found dead."

"That's interesting. Do you have any idea how she could have been out of her room? It doesn't sound like she could have gone unnoticed, but yet she did."

"Kellie liked to smoke and that was another rule I had set. No smoking in the room. I had been through a fire before and wasn't about to go through that again. She would sometimes go out back after room check and light up, but she usually had Tony with her," she told Harry.

"Was Tony with her the night she disappeared?" Harry asked her, and motioned for Tom to fill his coffee cup.

"Would you like a coffee, Millie?" Harry offered.

"No thanks, Harry. What I would like is to go and get breakfast and then to check on my girls. Why don't we go and do that, then I can introduce you to my girls and you can ask them any questions. Breakfast can even be my treat."

Looking at Tom who shrugged his shoulders, Harry asked Carl if he wanted to go to breakfast with them.

"Sure," Carl said.

"Looks like we're going to take you up on your offer Millie," Harry told her, getting up from his chair and motioning toward the door.

As they made their way to breakfast, just a few short miles from town, the screams that were filling the inside of the root cellar torture room were coming to an end.

Soon the tongue would be cut out and Lui Chang would drown as her lungs filled up with her own blood and suffocate her to death.

CHAPTER 6

Lui Chang was close to the end of her existence here on this earth. Her young body was screaming out in pain, as the white hot branding iron was pressed onto her left breast.

As her eyes clouded over on the brink of passing out, cold water splashed against her face, robbing her of the comfort of a deep, painless sleep.

Through her pain-raked eyes, Lui Chang stared into the laughing face of her tormentor whose laugh she couldn't hear above her scream.

Lui Chang felt the hand kneading the seared flesh that had just been branded and the pain was doubled. She fought against the ropes that bound her hands and feet in a frail attempt to get unbound. Through her pain-filled eyes, Lui Chang saw the lips of the man who was causing her such great pain start to move, but heard no voice. The sheer volume of her screams had shattered her eardrums.

The room was suddenly filled with a bright light, ten times brighter than the light from the noon-day sun. Gone too, were the moving lips of her tormentor, replaced by a hundred moving lips from the smiling faces of a multitude of angels.

Lui Chang would cheat her tormentor the pleasure of watching her any longer undergo the last of his deeds.

The cold water being splashed onto her was replaced by the coolness of a blanket of clouds engulfing her tender, naked body with layer after layer of soft, cool cloth which would be her dress from now through the eternities.

She would watch from the heavens as the last deeds from this sick, sick man was performed on her flesh. She would watch as her body was removed from the root cellar and wrapped in some kind of blanket, and in the blackness of the night was dumped in the alley that, just a few hours earlier, was alive with those looking for clues that might help tell them who the killer of Cinnamon Hollow's Painted Ladies was.

"Sheriff, sheriff, come quickly," the young voice of Billy Joe burst through the wildly swung opened door to the office as he came charging through it.

"Come quickly," he said again, rushing back to the opened door and frantically pointing in the direction of the alley across the street.

Tom, who had been standing next to the stove, about to pour a coffee, was the first one through the door behind Billy Joe. Carl and Harry followed.

Following them to the alley, he noticed there were several of the town's people standing around at the entrance to the alley. Approaching, Harry saw the bloody, naked body of a woman lying on a blanket in the dirt. Tom was already kneeling next to her about ready to pick her up in his arms.

"Stop!" Harry shouted, giving him just enough time to grab Tom and pull him away from the body.

"It's Lui Chang, Harry," Tom told him, his voice cracking as his body was racked with the first signs of horror at who he was gazing upon.

Suddenly stepping away, Tom's stomach could no longer contain last night's meal. The desire to go to Tom's side was great, but Harry knew Tom needed this time to himself, besides, he didn't need someone standing by his side at this particular moment.

"All of you people, please stay back away from the alley," Harry instructed them. Taking off his hat, he placed it over her womanhood to shield her from the many sets of eyes wanting to glimpse her naked form.

"Carl, would you stand over there and keep those people away," Harry asked him before realizing he was already starting to do just that.

I like that Carl. Harry thought to himself. Wonder if he ever thought of becoming a US Marshal?

Turning in the direction of Tom, Harry saw the mayor, Dwayne, approaching.

"Oh no! Not another one!" he exclaimed through a high shrill voice, approaching Harry.

"It's okay, Mayor," Harry informed him, looking in his direction and noticing that several more townspeople had arrived trying to get a look at the body lying in the alley.

"Sheriff Tom," Harry heard the voice call out. "Sheriff Tom," it repeated.

"Not now, Two Shots," Harry heard Tom reply.

Peculiar name for a person. Harry thought, but knew there was some hidden meaning that went along with it.

"Mayor, why don't you go and get the Doc and have him come here, along with the undertaker. Let's get this body out of here and away from all these people."

"Sure will, Harry," he said, heading toward the crowd of people at the alley's entrance. Harry also noticed that the one who was called 'Two Shots' by Tom, was walking away.

The mayor was only gone a few minutes when he returned, out of breath, along with the Doc and the undertaker.

"Carl, go get your notepad and come back here." Harry instructed.

"I need you to do a quick look over the body, Doc, before we move her to where you can do a better examination, but let's wait till Carl returns."

When Carl returned, he stepped up next to the three of them.

"Okay, Harry," he said. In return, Harry told the Doc to begin by telling them what he was seeing.

"This girl is younger than the past ones and is of Oriental descent. Looking at her nude body and the wounds on it, I'd say she underwent some torture," he whispered.

"By the marks on her wrist and ankles, she was bound to something. The marks are different on each one. If they were bound together they would be the same," he continued.

There was a crowd of people now, so Harry told the Doc, as much as Harry hated to, they would need to move the body and finish up in his office.

"Mayor, will you get a couple of guys and let's move her over to Doc's office," Harry told Dwayne.

"Carl, you go with them. Tom, you stay here with me for a few minutes."

"Okay folks. There is nothing more to see here, so let's go about your business now," Tom said.

As everyone slowly departed when the body was removed, Harry couldn't help but notice the look on Tom's face. He was using all his inner strength to keep his composure after having seen what he just did.

"We'll get this guy, Tom," Harry promised, laying his hand on Tom's shoulder. "But right now, we have more work to do."

Tom just nodded his head in agreement.

"I'll be okay, Harry," Tom said, taking a deep breath. "What's next?"

"Who was that man who called to you from the crowd?" Harry asked.

"The town drunk. Everyone knows him as 'Two Shots' cause he never orders just a shot, but always two."

"We need to talk to him. He seemed like he had something important to say. Has he had any information on the other killings?" Harry asked Tom.

"No. As a matter of fact, this is the first time I've seen Two Shots in some time."

"Let's go over to Doc's office and see what he has discovered, then get Carl and come back here."

Two important things they learned from Doc was, Lui Chang hadn't had her breast cut off or her tongue cut out like the rest had, but she had been tortured in the same manor. She had several cuts along her body as well as cigarette burns, and several 'W' branding marks, all in the same places as the others.

The other difference being the smile upon her face. Where the others all had a look of terror, she had a smile.

"That smile seems odd. Don't you think, Harry?"

"It does, that's for sure Tom, but I have a theory," Harry told them. "And I just might be right."

"You have all of our attention, Harry. We're all ears."

"I think the smile and the fact she hadn't had her breast and tongue cut off was she probably died before he was able to inflict these last two things. The smile was her way of showing that she had cheated him out of this final stage of torture. That's why he didn't continue with his regular pattern. There was no need for him to. She was dead and wouldn't be able to give him any more enjoyment, so he stopped."

"That sure makes a lot of sense, Harry," Doc said.

Giving everyone a few minutes to take that all in, Harry continued.

"The killer has been very meticulous in not leaving anything at his dump site, except this time he left the victim laying on a blanket. Why?"

"Maybe he did feel some remorse for this one; seeing she up and died on him, denying him all of his pleasure," Tom injected.

"What's your take on that blanket? It looks like it might have been expensive," Harry picked up a corner of the blanket and rubbed it between his fingers.

"Judging by its condition and the feel of the material, it's not very old," Harry informed those there.

Amanda had been showing Harry some of the difference in material because he had mentioned her dress once and how nicely it fit her compared to some he had seen on other women. It was then she started pointing out the different material. Its coarseness, softness, even color to tell if it was new, fairly new, or well worn.

This blanket was fairly new. Harry thought.

Thinking back to earlier that morning, Harry looked at Tom and asked him about that man who tried to get his attention.

"Why don't you go and locate this Two Shots and bring him to the office, so that we can talk to him. He seemed like whatever he had to say was important."

"Like I told you earlier, I hadn't seen Two Shots in some time, but will search for him and bring him in so we can talk to him," having said that, Tom left.

The day was hot and Tom went to all the saloons and checked out the horse stalls at the livery stable where Two Shots was known to pass out.

Checking the loft, Tom found Two Shots passed out. He had made a space out of hay, where he couldn't be seen unless someone was searching the loft. Tom couldn't help but notice the odor coming from Two

Shots. A mixture of alcohol, vomit and the strong smell of urine.

After much shaking, Tom got a rise out of Two Shots. Getting him down from the loft was no easy chore, but Tom got it done.

"Where we going, sheriff?" Two Shots asked. His speech was distorted from the amount of booze he had consumed.

"Well, I was going to take you to my office, but think you need a bath and a change of clothes first."

Tom could almost be sick with his smell, but managed to get him to the bath house run by Ling Sue who owned the place. Although Ling Sue had owned the place for as long as Tom could remember, she didn't speak English. Along with the bath house, she ran a laundry and had a girl who had a handcart full of clothes, which she sold in the streets.

It was this handcart that caught Tom's attention, as he led Two Shots in the direction of the bath house.

"What do you say, Two Shots. Want some new duds?" Tom asked. Without waiting for an answer, Tom changed direction and now headed toward the cart and some clean clothes for Two Shots. Finding a shirt and a pair of trousers, Tom paid for them and now they headed to the bath house.

"I need a drink," Two Shots told Tom. Breaking from his grasp, he headed toward the closest saloon, but was stopped by Tom's strong grasp again on his arm.

Once at the bath house, Ling Sue took the two-bits from Tom for Two Shots bath and having his old clothes washed. Twenty minutes passed, then Two Shot emerged smelling much better and wearing the new duds Tom had purchased for him. Two Shots wanted a drink, but Tom steered him away from the saloons and to his office.

Harry introduced himself and nodded in Carl's direction so that his presence was known. Carl just tipped his head as he knew Two Shots and had nothing good to say about the town's drunkard.

"Would you like a cup of coffee," Harry offered him. He shook his head no.

"I could really use a drink though," he returned.

"Let's talk first, then we will see about a drink," Harry told him. This brought a smile to his face.

"You were outside of the alley when the body of one of the town's Painted Ladies was discovered today," Harry's statement brought a nod from him.

"You tried to get Tom's attention and when he told you later, you walked away."

Again, Two Shots nodded in agreement.

"Well, Two Shots, you're here now so why don't you tell us what it was you wanted to say this morning?" Harry asked.

With his head hung low, and in a whispered voice he said, "I recognized something."

"Go on, Two Shots, tell us what it was you recognized?"

Harry could tell, if he wanted information, well, he needed to ask direct questions and not to expect Two Shots to volunteer any information.

"The blanket," was all he answered.

"What about the blanket," Harry asked, wondering how he could possibly have anything to tell Harry concerning it that would reflect on this case.

"I've seen it before," he answered Harry.

"Tell me all you know about that blanket?" Harry told him. "Where did you see it, how many times have you seen it, how do you know it's the same blanket?"

"I have one just like it," he told Harry, raising his head up so he was looking Harry right in the eyes. "And I know where there are more just like it."

The quietness in the room up till then was shattered by everyone's, "What?" Hearing what Two Shots had just said.

It's hard to comprehend that this little man, the town's drunk, could become the town's hero by solving this case. Harry thought. Knowing it wouldn't be the first time a nobody had solved an important case.

"Where did you see these blankets?" Tom questioned, not being able to contain himself.

It was here that Two Shots did what any other drunk would do knowing he had some information you were looking for.

"Buy me a bottle and not only will I tell ya, I'll show ya."

"I usually don't play these games. Instead, I would throw you in jail," Harry told him, but, if you show us where we can find more blankets just like this one, well, I'll buy you a bottle and a comfortable room to enjoy it in." Harry told him, overlooking the scowls Harry was receiving from Tom.

"That's a deal, Marshal," he said, getting up from his chair so fast it startled Carl who tossed his notepad into the air.

"You all coming," he said already at the office door. "It's not far from here. We can walk it, if you want."

As they walked from the office, the short hairs once again raised up on the back of Harry's neck as a danger signal. Automatically, his eyes turned towards the alley, but saw no one.

About the time Harry felt the hairs on his neck rise up, the eyes that had been watching the sheriff's office when they stepped outside disappeared into the shadows.

"Something wrong, Harry?" It was Tom's voice. He had turned around just as Harry had stopped and saw a concerned look on his face.

"Just had one of those feelings, Tom. C'mon let's get going before Carl and Two Shots out pace us."

They didn't know it, but this case was about to get interesting.

Chapter 7

"I thought you said it was a short walk?" Harry questioned Two Shots.

"Not much further now. Just up around the bend in the road."

"The only thing that is around the bend is the old abandoned Wright's farm," Tom whispered. "Nobody has lived there for a long time."

Wright farm! That might just be the lead to the "W" that all the dead women were branded with. This is going to be the break in this case that I was sure would turn up, Harry thought.

"Wright's farm!" exclaimed Tom moments after saying the name out loud. "Could that be what the "W" stood for on those dead Painted Ladies?" It was as much of a statement as a question.

I was right in my assessment of Tom. He was a smart person and would make a good US Marshal. I will need to talk to him, when this case is done. Harry thought

"There it is!" exclaimed Two Shots, quickening his step. "That's the place I was telling you about."

"What happened to the folks who lived there?" Harry questioned Tom.

"I can only tell you what I have heard tell about them," answered Tom.

"Tell me later. Right now let's see what Two Shots has to offer."

"In here," Two Shots pointed out.

The door to the abandoned farmhouse was open, so they went inside. Except for animal droppings all over the place, it was pretty much in the same condition it was left in.

"Nobody has ransacked the place," Harry stated. "Most abandoned homes would have been trashed by local kids or other passerbys."

"Place is haunted!" exclaimed Two Shots. "Sometimes in the dark of the evening, a light can be seen moving about from room to room," he continued. "What I want to show you though is upstairs and then out back."

Upstairs in one of the bedrooms at the foot of the bed was a chest that Two Shots went over to and raised the lid.

Inside the chest were several items, two of which were identical blankets to the one that Lui Chang was found in the alley laying on. Tom took out the two blankets, which were neatly folded and laid them on the bed.

Opening one up he remarked. "Sure does look like the blanket we have, Harry."

"It sure does at that," Harry had to agree. "Feels like it to," Harry continued, running his hand over the material.

"It doesn't appear anyone has been staying in this room," Harry concluded. "Let's check out the rest of the house."

Walking from room to room, Harry once again felt the short neck hairs rise up.

"What's the matter, Harry?" asked Tom, seeing a different look come over Harry's face and saw his body kind of freeze up.

Harry explained to Tom this sixth sense he had developed over time and told him he really felt like there were eyes watching them.

"For sure, no one is in here Harry," Tom said.

"I've had this feeling several times now, so let's tell Carl and Two Shots to be all eyes from here on out. I can't ignore this feeling. I know someone is watching us from somewhere."

Outside, along the tree line, was a set of eyes glued to a pair of field glasses. The same set of eyes that had watched from the alley and later on from the rooftop of the mercantile store. He had watched as the town drunk was taken in by Tom and then watched as he had lead the marshal and sheriff along with the newspaperman Carl to the abandoned farm and will probably discover the root cellar and the horrors that the walls there had witnessed.

Sure enough, ten minutes after entering the farmhouse, the four walked back out through the front door and headed towards the back yard and to the root cellar.

"Let me tell you a story," Two Shots said as they walked towards the large mound of dirt and to the door that enclosed the cellar.

In a whispered voice, Two Shots started to tell his tale which he had been holding inside for some time now.

"I started coming here about two months ago," he began. "I was drunk one night and stumbled out of town and found myself here, at the front door of the farmhouse. It was raining and I pounded on the door, but no one answered. Finally, I guess I hit the door too hard and it opened."

Everyone stood and listened without interruption as Two Shots told his tale.

"Once inside, I crawled over into a corner and passed out, awoke the next morning, wondering just where the hades I was. I walked around inside, checking out every room. That's where I saw the blankets and I also took some clothes I found in one of the closets. I started staying there and one morning I woke up to the sound of footsteps downstairs. I was in the room where the chest with the blankets was."

"What's that?" Carl suddenly questioned.

"What's what?" Harry asked, feeling the hairs rise on his neck once more.

"Over there," he said, pointing to the tree line about one-hundred yards away. "I thought I caught a quick flash of light. Like the reflection of the sun off a mirror."

Having looked in the direction he pointed, Harry made a mental note as to the location, so it could be checked out later.

"Go on with your story," Harry told Two Shots.

"When I heard the footsteps, I crawled under the bed just in case whoever it was came upstairs, but whoever it was, never did."

"Did you see who it was?" asked Tom.

"No, not really. Once I heard the footsteps leave, I crawled from under the bed and peeked out the window just in time to see the backside of a man walking towards town, but there was something in his walk that looked familiar. I just don't know."

"That's good Two Shots. If you recall anything more you come find Tom or myself, okay?"

Two Shots nodded his head in agreement.

Getting back to the business at hand, Harry reached out to open the door to the root cellar and saw there was a padlock on it. Not an old rusted one which you would have figured one to be, but a fairly new one.

Who would put a lock on a root cellar of an old abandoned farm? Harry thought. Even the door looked newer, like it had been made recently.

"It's locked Harry," said Tom. "Who would put a lock on a root cellar?"

"My thoughts exactly, Tom. Let's get this door open!" Harry exclaimed, looking around for something to break or pry the lock apart with.

'Boooom' a loud shot rang out. At the same time, Harry heard the sound of metal and wood being shattered.

Facing the door, Harry saw Tom had taken out his pistol and had blasted away at the lock, splintering the wood around it.

"That should do it Harry," Tom said. He grabbed a hold of the shattered lock and twisted it. It fell from its latch leaving the door ready to be opened.

The sickening odor of death came rushing out from the root cellar as the door was opened. There was no doubt as to what they were about to find, they were just not prepared to witness the extent of what this find would be. The smell of burnt flesh was the strongest smell.

From the light of the opened door, Tom saw a lantern. Retrieving it, he lit it and when he did, the room came alive.

No one spoke a word. It was like they had stepped onto hallowed ground. It would be several minutes before anyone even dared to take a big breath.

"Oh my God!" exclaimed Carl, who was the first to say anything. "What have we discovered?"

The light from the lantern had exposed all the gruesome instruments of torture and death. A metal bed was in the center of the room. Attached to the head and foot boards were strips of rawhide that were used for the purpose of securing someone's hands and feet. Under closer examination, you could see the dark stains of blood on them.

In one corner was an open fire pit. Laid into it were two long iron handles, which when removed, exposed what everyone there knew they would. The 'W' of the branding irons.

"There is still some warmth in this pit," Harry whispered, having extracted one of the branding irons and feeling its warmth.

Along the bed was a half full bucket of water containing a dipper. On the dirt floor were a multitude of cigarette butts which were used to inflict pain as they burned into the warm, tender flesh of the victim. There were two chairs in the room which seemed odd to Harry.

On one of the chairs were two neatly folded blankets just like the ones found in the farmhouse and with the body of Lui Chang.

"This is the place, isn't it Harry?" Tom spoke after several minutes.

"It would appear to be, Tom," Harry replied, picking up a long bladed knife as sharp as a razor.

Having witnessed the removal of breast and tongue of several of the women, one knew exactly what it was used for.

"I need a drink!" It was Two Shots voice that echoed into the room, breaking the silence which had overtaken everyone.

Having seen enough, Harry motioned for everyone to vacate the cellar. The fresh air of the outside was welcomed and you could hear the deep breaths from everyone as they tried to clear their lungs of the deadly air of the cellar.

"Carl, would you take Two Shots back to town and get him his much needed drink? Tom and I are going to go see what made that flash you saw earlier."

"Sure will, Harry. I'll meet you two back at the office. I want to write down all that we saw here today."

As gruesome as the sights were here today, there was excitement in Carl's voice.

I can only imagine the story brewing inside his head, Harry thought as he watched the two head for town.

"Seeing we have without a doubt discovered where the victims were tortured and killed, do you suppose he will stop now? He will know right away when he comes back and finds the root cellar has been broken into."

"I sure hope so," Harry told Tom. But nothing says that will be the case. "If he is intent on continuing to kill, he will find other outlets to do it."

At the end of the field where the wood line begins, Tom and Harry found a makeshift blind. Probably used for hunting so a deer wouldn't see you. In this case, to hide a person from being exposed as he spied on them.

Tom noticed a path that entered the blind from the rear.

"Where do you suppose this path leads to, Harry?"

"I don't know Tom, but let's find out," Harry said, stepping past him and following the path he had pointed out.

Once in the woods, the path branched out into several ones. Following each took some time, but each one led back to the farmhouse or to the road into town. Two actually led to the outskirts of town, and although hidden, were marked by a large boulder and a big cottonwood tree.

One of the paths that went from the farmhouse to the outskirts of town was more pronounced than the others, leading Harry to believe it was made by dragging a body across it.

This one path was the one marked by the large boulder and that is where they found another makeshift blind. No doubt used to hide in and to observe the town.

Anyone could walk right upon it and not recognize it. Here was the only place where they found some signs of a woman being there. Found were several long strands of hair that were obviously a woman's. Finding those strands of hair brought into reality all of the findings from the day.

As if both Tom and Harry were thinking the same thing, both stood quietly and bowed their heads.

"We need to find this person," Harry whispered to Tom. "Two Shots is our best answer. He needs to remember."

Neither Tom nor Harry saw the flash of light coming from the church's steeple. Once again, a set of eyes were glued to the field glasses observing their every move.

Chapter 8

Tom, Carl, and Harry sat back in the office discussing the finds of the day over a fresh pot of coffee.

"Do you think they should stake out the farmhouse and root cellar just in case someone shows up back there?" questioned Tom.

"I don't think that will be necessary, Tom," Harry told him. "Whoever it is already knows he has been found out. I believe he was there today and observed the making of this day. No, I don't believe we need to watch that place right now."

"Where is Two Shots?" asked Tom.

"I bought him a bottle and left him in the saloon. That man was one happy camper. His grin was from ear to ear when the bartender sat that whiskey bottle down in front of him with an empty shot glass."

"Did he have anything more to say on the walk to town?" Harry asked. "I would bet he knows who he saw," Harry continued. "I'd place money on it."

"Well, if he did, he wasn't saying. Matter of fact, he didn't utter a word," Carl told them.

"Don't you find that a little strange?" Harry asked. "I would have been a chatter box having seen what he saw, and more so, knowing he had probably seen the person responsible for all these killings."

"Only thing I noticed was him looking around the room when we entered the saloon as though he was looking for someone. Other than that, nothing," Carl continued.

"I'm about ready to put this day to bed and go get some supper. Who wants to join me?"

"I'll join you Harry," said Tom.

"How can either of you eat after what we saw today?" Carl asked. "Not me, that's for damn sure. I'm heading home."

"Let's stop by the saloon on the way just to check up on Two Shots," Harry said to Tom. "If there was someone there today observing us, that person knows it must have been Two Shots who brought us there, otherwise why would he be there."

Harry's gut feeling was to be concerned for Two Shots. After supper, he wanted to check in with Rosy, Millie, and Sing Lin to see if any of their girls had heard anything new.

"Do you think the killer will strike again?" Tom asked, as we sat eating.

"Hard to say," Harry answered. "I'm almost one hundred percent sure he saw us today and if I'm correct he won't dare to, or he just might have the gumption to do just that. Either way, his days are numbered," he told Tom. "Just need another piece to this puzzle."

"How could a human being do such horrible doings to another human being, much less to a defenseless woman?" Tom whispered as we finished eating and were outside walking towards Millie's establishment.

"Whoever it is, Tom, I feel he is reliving something in his own life which is so embedded into his mind that he can't tell the difference between his life and that which he is creating with his torture and butchery."

"That smell of burnt flesh in the root cellar was overwhelming Harry," Tom continued speaking as they walked. "The pain inflected by that branding iron is almost too much to imagine."

"Keep that thought fresh in your mind for now, Tom. It will help keep this mission fresh in your mind and will keep you going when you're feeling like you just can't go on."

"Sounds to me like experience talking Harry," Tom noted.

"That it is, Tom. The trail gets lonesome and downright tiring at times, to the point you just want to give up and take a break, but you know you can't. There's a bad guy out there, and if you lose sight of that, he will continue being a bad guy. It's up to you to see he is captured and punished for his crimes."

Stepping inside Millie's, the first thing Harry noticed was the smell of the place.

Cigarette and cigar smells were replaced by those of lavender, vanilla, and an assortment of flower smells. There was no smoking in Millie's place.

Next, was the décor. The brightly painted walls, plush seating, carpeted flooring, beautiful hanging pictures, and the lighting was almost too bright for the eyes.

"What's with the lighting, Harry?" a blinking Tom asked.

"Not really sure, Tom," Harry replied, his own eyes straining against the light.

Next were the girls or better said, women. Millie had no girls, but only attractive women in their late twenties and dressed in bright colored dresses that were cut to expose and enhance the female form. They were moving about the room going from table to table as a piano player was playing some ragtime tune. There wasn't a seated bar, but individual tables and several booths.

There were several males seated and drinking from nice glasses. Not the odd stuff you were used to seeing in most saloons, but nice crystal.

A flash of light coming from one of the tables caught Tom's attention.

"Did you see that flash of light just now?" he asked. "It was just like that flash of light I saw earlier today, while we were at the farmhouse."

"No, I didn't see it," Harry replied. Knowing that the flash Tom had just seen was that of the bright light reflecting off someone's glass told Harry the flash he had seen earlier was probably off the lens of a field glass.

"Sheriff Tom, and US Marshal Harry Finch," came Millie's voice from behind them.

Millie had been out and was just returning. The couple of items she had in her hands, she handed to her bartender.

"What brings you two here?" she asked, stepping in front of them and turning to face them as she spoke.

"We were just dropping by to check up on everything and to see if you might have heard anything more from any of your girls," Harry told her. "Plus, I have a couple more questions to ask you."

Having said that, Harry noticed the music had stopped and the room was now quiet as all eyes were staring at them. Millie turned and with a wave of her hand, the piano player once again put fingers to ivory and the room came alive with a peppy number.

"Let's take a seat," she said, and pointed to an empty booth. "Would either of you like a drink?" she asked, knowing quite well that neither Tom nor Harry would drink while on business.

Once seated she asked, "What is it you wanted to ask me?"

"Have you seen or heard anything new since the newest body has been found? Anything at all?" Harry asked.

"Nothing, Harry. I told you if I hear anything I would let you know," she answered, sounding a little annoyed, not only by the question, but his and Tom's presence in her place.

"I need for both of you to swear that if you see a familiar face in here, it goes no further. My girls cater to businessmen, married men, and even a couple of the town's fathers who have never had to worry about anyone spilling the beans on them, either with their wives, or the newspaper," Millie told them.

"You can assure your customers their goings on are safe with us," Harry told her. "We have no interest in that matter, unless you are suspicious of someone."

"If there is nothing else, Harry. I need to greet my guests. They like it when I stop by their table for some chit chat," Millie said, rearranging her assets and putting a wicked looking smile on her face.

"One more thing," Harry said, placing his hand on her arm, so she sat back down. "Did you know the family who lived in the abandoned farmhouse just outside of town?"

"If you're talking about Willard Wright's place, I don't know much Harry, other than what I've heard. They had been gone for some time, before I came to town. They were a strange family from what I've been told."

"I've heard that same thing, but no one has any facts to tell me, other then what you just said," Harry told her. "Why were they considered a strange family?

"I need to find out what happened to them. Where did they go? Exactly when did they leave? And more importantly, why did they leave and not take any of their things? The inside of the farmhouse looked like they just walked out and not bothered to take anything with them."

"I will ask around if you want me to, Harry," Millie said. "I can have my girls ask around also. Most of their customers are long time town folk."

"Thanks for the offer, but I don't want to stir up anything right now as to who we suspect the killer might be. What I need from you is to make sure your girls are overly cautious for now," Harry told her. "Just continue keeping your eyes and ears open for anything out of the ordinary."

As they got up from the table, Harry complimented her on a beautiful place.

"Why, thank you Harry. I try to give my customers a taste of the good life which some are accustomed to anyways."

"Thank you again," Harry told her, tipping his hat and giving the place a last look around before stepping outside into the heat of early evening once again.

Someone has to know about the Wright family. Harry told himself. Now to go and talk with Rose again. Maybe she will have some information on the Wright family.

* * * * *

"Harry!" It was the mayor's voice. He had just stepped out of the general store and was sucking on a peppermint stick.

"Mayor," Harry nodded his head, and at the same time reached out his hand for a cordial hand shake. "I was just going to Rosy's, but seeing you're here, I have a question for you."

"Anything Harry."

"Let's go over to the office. Carl should be there. I want us all to hear what you might have to say."

Several people said hello to the mayor on their way to the office and he was quick to brush off any mention of the killings.

"Mayor," it was Carl who spoke first as we stepped into the office. Catching Harry's eye, Tom indicated the pot of coffee to which Harry nodded he would like a cup. The steaming hot coffee arrived at Harry's desk just as he sat down.

The hot, black liquid had a soothing effect on him after the day they had just experienced.

"I asked the mayor here so I might get a couple questions answered, but before we start, I want to say once again that what we talk about here stays here for now. No mention of what we discuss is brought up outside these walls unless otherwise asked by me. We all understand that, correct?" Harry said.

All heads nodded in agreement.

"Okay then. Mayor, what can you tell us about the Wright family who used to live in the farm just outside of town?"

"You're talking about Willard Wright's place? Strange lot they were," he told them.

"I've heard they were a strange family, now tell me what made them strange in your recollection of them?" Carl said.

"Well, let's see. There were five members to the family, mom and dad, two girls and a boy. They would come into town as a family and were very quiet. Never said hello to anyone. Wouldn't even speak to the clerk at the general store, but picked out their own stuff and paid for it, never once saying a word."

"Maybe they couldn't speak," Harry told him. "There have been families who were considered deaf and dumb and couldn't speak. That isn't unheard of," Harry continued.

"They all could talk. I heard them myself."

"Tell us more," Harry said, motioning to Tom he'd like another cup of coffee.

"Well, one morning I decided to go fishing. I had a taste for some brook trout. Down at the creek is a spot that was dammed up creating a large pool. The local kids go swimming there sometimes, also a great place to fish. Well, this morning as I approached the pool, I heard voices and people splashing around in the water. It was the Wright kids. They were swimming in their undergarments, splashing about and hollering to each other. As I said, they can talk."

"What else can you tell us about that family?" Harry asked, wanting to know more.

"From where I was, I could clearly see all three kids bore a multitude of scars on their backs and also on the other parts of their bodies. As hard as it was to look at, greater was knowing how painful it must have been on their young bodies to receive them. As I watched, the boy suddenly grabbed one of the girls by the hair and dragged her out of the water. I watched as he slapped her around some, before having her kneel, at which time he picked up a small switch and started whipping her with it, all the time laughing at hearing her scream."

They all sat there in silence, as the mayor recalled what he had seen that day concerning the Wright kids.

"How old were the kids?" Harry asked, when the mayor had stopped talking for a minute.

"Probably in their late teens or there about," was his answer.

Carl was writing just as fast as he could, not wanting to miss a word.

"Oh my god!" Dwayne suddenly exclaimed. The expression on his face was ghostly. The look of someone who had just seen something so horrible it hurt to think it, and that pain showed on his face.

"What is it mayor?" Harry asked, taken in by Dwayne's sudden outburst.

It took him a moment before he could speak, then he started, and something in Harry's brain told him exactly what they were about to hear.

"The sister to the one being whipped, went out of the water and rushed up to her side, just as I thought she was going to grab her brother's arm, instead, she reached down and pulled her sister's undergarment down to expose her flesh to the switch. That's when I saw it. There on her bottom cheek was a massive scar in the shape of a 'W' where she had been branded."

After the sounds of everyone taking in a sharp breath, the quietness in the room could have been cut with a knife. The quiet lasted several minutes before Tom stood and walked to the stove and picked up the coffee pot.

"Anyone like a coffee?"

Tom's question was met by shaken heads as no one chose to speak.

"Continue when you can," Harry whispered, now wanting to hear the rest of his story.

"All the time he was whipping her, he was shouting, 'scream, scream' and she did as the switch fell across bare skin. Even from my distance, you could make out the thin red lines the switch was leaving on her pink skin."

"How long did he continue beating his sister?" Harry asked, motioning to Tom that he would like a coffee now.

"It would have probably gone on longer if it hadn't been for his father's voice calling out to him."

Here it is. The moment we have all been waiting for! Will this name be that of our killer of the town's Painted Ladies? This thought exploded through Harry's mind as he waited, like all of them, for the mayor to say the name.

"Tony," he finally said out loud. "That's the name I heard being called," he told us.

It was another several minutes before anyone in the room spoke.

"I don't know why I hadn't remembered all that until now," Dwayne said. "Tony Wright. Do you suppose he is our killer?" Dwayne asked, sitting there with head bowed, shaking it slowly.

"Well, we can't rule out him or the father," Harry told him. "Where is the family now? Their farm is abandoned. How long has it been since they lived there?" These were the next rush of questions Harry needed answered.

"I can shine some light on those questions," the mayor continued. "The picture will become a lot clearer."

"We're all ears, mayor," Harry told him.

"The Wright farm has been abandoned now for about five years. It was after the discovery of the bodies of Willard, his wife and a grave that the place became abandoned. The grave was dug up and a body of a young girl was what they found buried in it.

"It's not real clear as to what happened, but it does point fingers at Tony and maybe his sister, but they were gone and never questioned. That's the story as I can remember it."

The tale he told of that day was unbelievable. Dwayne continued.

"One day a passerby stopped in at the Wright place and seeing no one around, knocked at their door. Getting no response and finding the door half open, he went inside.

"Finding no one in the farmhouse, he walked around outside, checking in the barn and then the root cellar. It was there he found Willard and his wife dead. They had both been severely beaten and stabbed many times. Later that day, the sheriff discovered a freshly dug grave, just outside of the root cellar.

"There were lots of stories going around and some of them were printed up in the newspaper, so I'm sure Carl, if you looked back through the papers archives, you should be able to find something."

"So, no one really knows what happened there?" Harry questioned.

"No, Harry. No one does, but this sure opens up a lot more questions, doesn't it?"

It sure does, that's for sure. Harry thought.

Chapter 9

Having heard the mayor's recollection of the Willard Wright family, it became clear to Harry that they needed to track down the son, Tony and maybe his sister, if they could get a name.

"Someone has to know who this family was and what became of Tony and his sister after the killing of his mom and dad and other sister," Harry said.

Harry's gut feeling told him, find Tony and he finds the killer.

Harry still felt like Two Shots was going to be a key in finding Tony, or at least, answering some of his questions.

"Tom. Go out and find Two Shots and bring him here. He knows more than what he told us I'm sure of it," Harry told him.

Harry extended his hand to Dwayne and thanked him for all his information and told him he could go about his business.

"If you think of anything else, mayor, let me know," Harry said as the mayor left the office.

"I'm gonna go search through all the old newsprint and see what I can find concerning the Wright family and their killing," said Carl, getting to his feet and following the mayor out the door.

Harry poured himself another coffee and sat back and waited on the return of Tom and Two Shots.

Wonder what Amanda is doing now. Harry thought, missing her and having a few minutes to think about her, then praying she is fine.

I think I'll send her a telegraph later. That thought brought a smile to Harry's face knowing that receiving a telegraph would bring one to hers. About one hour passed before Tom returned and he was alone

"Where's Two Shots?" Harry asked him when he entered the office alone.

"I looked all over and he was nowhere to be found," he told Harry. "No one has seen him."

"Carl brought him to town this morning and left him with a bottle at Sally's place. I figured you would find him passed out there or someplace else. Did you check the livery stables?"

"Sally's was the last place anyone had seen him. Sally herself had spoken to him, because he was causing a small ruckus with the piano player," he told Harry. "He got up and left shortly after."

"Did Sally tell you what the ruckus between him and the piano player was about?" Harry asked, a little note of concern in his voice that matched the gnawing in his gut.

"She didn't know. When she asked Fingers, he told her he had too much to drink and complained about the song he was playing."

"Did she have anything more to say? Anything else take place before he left the place?"

"That was all she told me, Harry. Two Shots left shortly after and everything was fine."

Something about Two Shots having words with the piano player didn't set right with Harry and he voiced his concern with those in the room.

"Two Shots, for as much as he drinks and having never seen him one hundred percent sober lately, has never caused any trouble, not even when he would get tossed out of one of the saloons," Tom said. "I've never had him in my jail cell."

"What's Two Shots real name?" Harry asked. "Anyone know?"

"That's a good one, Harry!" exclaimed Tom. "Only know him by Two Shots. Never asked him his name. Basically I know nothing about him."

"Tom! You're the sheriff of this town and you don't know anything about the town's drunk? He should be the one person you know everything about. Just look! We have learned more about who the killer might be in the last few hours and that information coming from the one person no one knows anything about. The town's drunk."

"I guess because he has never been a problem or in any trouble, I have never felt the need to know anything about him," Tom spoke in his own defense. "Same with the Wright family."

"Another example, Tom!" Harry knew his tone of voice was chastising and he probably sounded more like a father scolding a son, than of a US Marshal talking to a lesser town sheriff.

"Everyone says they were a strange family, yet no one can give me a good example of why they were considered strange except for the mayor! No one, including yourself can even give me their names!" Harry said.

Relax, calm down. The voice inside Harry's head was telling him. Tom has a lot to learn. You can't speak to him using this tone of voice in front of others.

Catching himself, Harry changed his tone of voice with Tom.

"Tom, why don't you go around to the different saloons and see if anyone has a name for Two Shots and while at Sally's, get me the name of her piano player and any other information she can tell you about him," Harry said.

As Tom was leaving the office, Harry changed his directive for Tom.

"Why don't you tell Sally to have him come to this office tomorrow morning around ten o'clock, that way if we have any other questions we can ask him at that time."

"Will do, Harry," came his reply. "I'll be back shortly. Anything else you want from me before I leave?"

"Well, why don't you tell everyone if they see Two Shots to have him come to the office also," Harry replied.

"Already going to do that, Harry. As a matter of fact, I just thought of a place he might be."

"Well, check it out, but be careful," Harry warned. "There is a killer out there who probably knows we are close on his tail and he will become dangerous to us now."

As much as Harry was hoping whoever the killer was that he would know by now they were onto him and he would just leave the county. Harry didn't want that. Harry didn't want him taking his killing ways to some other town. No, Harry wanted him right here. If Harry's hunch about this person was correct, he would strike again, and when he did, Harry would be there.

"You've been pretty quiet, Carl," Harry said after Tom had left. "Do you know anything about Two Shots or the Wright family?"

"No I don't Harry, but all this gives me a really good idea to present to the mayor and also a really good addition to not only the town of Cinnamon Hollow, but also for my paper."

The excitement in his voice made Harry question what he had in mind.

"Well, with the mayor's approval, I'd like to organize a Saturday night, good old fashioned "Ho Down" for the entire town. It could be a pot luck supper with fiddle playing and foot stomping music where everyone could come and meet their neighbors."

Taking a minute to organize his thoughts he continued.

"It could even have a name. "Meet and Greet. How's that sound, Harry?"

Harry watched as Carl scribbled Meet and Greet on the pad he was writing on.

"By golly, Carl. I do believe you might be onto something there," Harry's voice sounding almost as excited as Carl's was. "Run that by the mayor for sure."

Harry made a mental note to make sure he added that idea to future towns Harry might be assigned to, if they didn't already have something like it.

"Getting back to your question, Harry. I could ask around to see what information I can get on Two Shots, the Wright family, and even Sally's piano player, if you'd like."

"No. Let's wait and see what Tom finds out," Harry told him. "I know you have other business to tend to, so if you want to leave, go ahead. I don't expect Tom back anytime soon. When he gets back, I'll send for you."

"Sounds good Harry," Carl said, walking to the door. "See you later."

Sitting alone in the quietness of the empty office, Harry had time to sort out the day's makings, feeling surer now than earlier that Two Shots held the key to who the killer was.

It was time again to call it a day and Tom hadn't returned.

"Where are you, Tom?" Harry said out loud. His voice echoing in the empty room.

Tom, not returning and it getting late, had Harry a little concerned but not overly. Tom had said he knew where he might find Two Shots, but gave no indication as to where that might be.

Locking the office, Harry made his way to Sally's where he now took most of his meals. The coffee was always fresh and hot and the meals tasty and of large portions.

Walking into Sally's, Harry caught Sally and saw her pick up a pot of coffee and a cup and motioned for Harry to follow her. A hot cup of coffee in front of Harry, Sally asked what he wanted and also if anyone was joining him.

"I haven't seen Tom all evening," Harry told her. "Has he been in here?"

"A little earlier," she told him. "I'll be right back with your order and we'll have a few minutes to sit and chat." With that, she was gone like the wind leaving Harry to his thoughts.

It wasn't long before a plate with a still sizzling T-bone steak on it, was placed in front of Harry. The aroma was invading his senses. Immediately, his taste buds were awakened and his mouth started to drool with anticipation.

"Smells delightful," Harry told her, "I haven't eaten anything today but drank a gallon of coffee," Harry continued.

"You need to eat, Harry," she told him, sounding just like Amanda did when she would tell him the same thing.

Cutting into the steak and taking the first bit was truly something to be enjoyed.

"One thing outside of a good cup of coffee is a great tasting steak, Sally, and yours is the best ever."

"Thank you, Harry. I don't recall anyone enjoying one of my steaks the way you do," she said with a smile on her face that could light up a room.

"You asked if I had seen Tom. He was in earlier looking for Two Shots and wanting some information on my piano player Fingers."

"Yes, I had him looking for Two Shots, and I heard he had some words with your piano player. Speaking of him, where is he?"

"He only plays here a couple times a week and then only during the day. He plays every evening at Millie's though. He should be over there right now," she told Harry.

"What's his real name?" Was his next question. "I know he is known by Fingers, but what's his given name?"

"I don't know," she answered, shrugging her shoulders, "but I know who might."

Turning towards the bar, she called out.

"Hey Billy. What's Fingers real name," she asked him.

"I don't know," he said. "Tommy, Teddy, Tony, something like that."

Tony! The name exploded inside Harry's head.

"Sorry he wasn't much help Harry," Sally told him. "I'll ask around some more."

Harry needed to get over to Millie's place, so he thanked Sally and left her place with his stomach full and his mind searching for more answers, hoping now Millie could answer some of Harry's questions. On his way to Millie's, Harry stopped by the office just in case Tom was there. He wasn't.

The first thing Harry noticed upon entering Millie's was there was no music playing. A quick glance at the piano, Harry saw an empty chair, and at the same time, Millie saw Harry.

The look on her face told Harry she wasn't happy to see him again inside her place. Harry could care less. He needed answers and by god he was going to get them. Millie was about to speak as she approached, but Harry spoke first.

"What's your piano player's name?" Harry asked, before she got a chance to speak.

"Fingers," she told him. "Now what's the meaning to all this?" She asked through clenched teeth. Obviously, she was not happy to see Harry inside her place again so soon.

"I know. Fingers is his nickname, but what's his given name, and where is he?"

As with earlier, the place became quiet as his presence was known and seconds after, there was movement in the room as the patrons got up and made a hasty exit not wanting to be seen.

"Tony," she told Harry. "Why all the interest in him? Tom was in earlier wanting to know the same thing."

"Where is he now?" Harry asked, not bothering to answer her question. "I don't see or hear him playing."

"He's not here, Harry," she told him. "Shortly after Tom spoke with him, he went outside to take his break, and when he returned, he told me he had to go because he wasn't feeling well. That was the last I saw of him." Her voice was a low whisper and her eyes scanned the room watching several patrons get up and leave.

"They'll be back as soon as I leave," Harry told her. "Do you know what Tony's last name is?"

"No I don't Harry, but I will find out for you. Come back in an hour or two. In the meantime, go ask Sally. Did you know he also plays piano and is a bouncer in her place, when not working here?"

"Yes, I did know that," and as a second thought asked, "Do you know who Two Shots is?"

"Yes!" she exclaimed, "Ben Horn. His sister was one of the killer's first victims, Kellie Horn who had worked for me about three years. Her death left him distraught and broken, even more then he already was," she told Harry, then continued.

"He used to come in from time to time, but was always drunk. Tony threw him out and he was barred from ever coming in again. After his sister's killing, he started drinking even more and was never seen sober. Kellie told me that he was her older brother and always gave her a hard time because of what she did for work. After her death, he swore he would kill whoever it was responsible."

"Ya! And he knows who that person is," Harry said under his breath and continued with, "where does Tony live?"

Chapter 10

As far as Harry was concerned, he knew who the killer was, Tony Wright, only thing now was finding him.

Where the hades is Tom? That was what Harry wanted to know. That was his thought upon leaving Millie's place.

Harry hadn't taken more than four steps when the hairs on his neck started to send out their familiar warning that danger lurked close by. There weren't any alleys to hide in, so his eyes looked up to the rooftops.

"I know you're out there," he whispered. His eyes, now a little more accustomed to the dark so at least Harry could make out the many roof lines. Many of which would make for good cover to hide behind if you wanted to watch someone without being seen. Also silhouetted against the night's sky was the church steeple, another excellent place for observation.

If I hurried towards the church, I could be there about the same time it would take a person to climb down from there. This being Harry's thought as to what to do, he took another few steps then turned towards the church and quickened his steps. Oblivious to anyone there in the steeple, he was headed towards them.

Making the decision to go around to the back of the church, as to going through the front door was a good decision, for there, just pushing open the back door was the person who must have been watching him.

"Hold it right there," Harry said in a loud voice. "Don't make me shoot you."

As the person stopped and turned in his direction, Harry was surprised at who was facing him.

"Della," was all Harry could murmur, so taken aback by seeing her.

"Don't shoot me, Harry," came her soft voice. "I don't have a gun."

Gone were the frilly clothes he had seen her in earlier on the stage, replaced by ordinary shirt and pants. Her hair tucked up and under an oversized cowboy hat. This part of the church faced a large boulder which Harry recognized as being one of those places that had a trail that would lead back to the Wright farm.

"You have a lot of talking to do," Harry said, taking her by the arm. "Let's go," he said, steering her towards the sheriff's office.

Not having Tom or Carl present, Harry decided to lock her up and question her in the morning when Carl and hopefully Tom would be here.

"Looks like you'll get to spend the night in jail," Harry told her, leading her into the sheriff's office and into the back room to the jail cell. Ignoring all her remarks, he locked the heavy iron cell door and left the cell room closing the door on his way out.

What do you make of all this now? Were his thoughts, as Harry hung the cell's door key on a hook behind his desk.

Where could Tom be? That was his thought stepping outside and locking the door behind him. Almost instantly, the hairs on the back of his neck alerted him to danger and Harry quickly glanced towards the alley.

For an instant, Harry caught the glow from a cigarette and knew someone was there in the shadows, watching. Harry also knew there was a hidden trail that lay just a few feet from the alley's entrance, but in the dark and not knowing the layout well enough, it would be difficult for him to find, but not for someone who had knowledge of the land. It would be here he needed to come in the morning.

After a restless night's sleep, Harry left his room and had a quick coffee before heading to the office.

"Tom," Harry shouted from afar, seeing him just getting ready to unlock the office door. "Where the tarnnation have you been?"

"I'll tell you when we get inside," his voice sounding a little shaky.

As soon as they entered, Della's voice could be heard and Tom gave me a quick, questionable look.

"I'll explain in a few minutes, for now put on some coffee," Harry told him, just as Carl came through the door.

"Tom!" he exclaimed. "We've been searching all over for you. Where you been?"

Carl's question went unanswered. Instead, the high, shrilled, voice of a female came through the cell room's door.

"You two don't look so surprised," Harry said, taking the keys and tossing them to Tom. "Go get our prisoner. She's probably about ready to wet herself."

A very loud, complaining woman was led from the cell room out into the office.

"Take her to the privy then bring her back here," Harry told Tom, noticing how different Della looked in these clothes.

"Who's that?" Carl asked as soon as they were gone.

"I'll tell you when they get back, but for now, finish making that pot of coffee Tom started, will ya?"

"Sure, sure, Harry," he replied, and with a smile on his face murmured. "This is going to be good."

It was easy to pick up on the excitement in his voice, after all, he was a writer and this sure would be some story.

You're gonna have one heck of a story to write once we're done here. Harry thought, feeling his own lips turn up into a small smirk.

The door opened and in flew Della followed by Tom, both were covered with dust.

"Git in there!" he yelled at her, continuing to push her into the cell room, where we all heard the metal door slam shut. Moments later he appeared and slammed the other door behind him also. Tossing the keys on the desk, rather the hanging them up, Tom just stood there shaking his head.

"She tried to run off," he said, and commenced brushing the dirt from his clothes.

"Who is she, Harry?" Tom asked, "and what is she doing in my jail?"

"Her name is Della DuPont, but before we get into all of what has transpired the last twenty-four hours, let's go get something to eat."

"What about Della?" Tom asked.

"We'll bring her back something," Harry told him. "Well maybe!" This he said with a grin.

As soon as they stepped outside, one of the town's kids came running up to them.

"Come quick!" he said, trying hard to catch his breath, then turning back around and headed off in the direction of the church.

Several people stood around in front of the church, while the reverend stood in front of the closed door. As we approached, he motioned for us to come his way.

"I found him here this morning," he told us, looking back over his shoulder as he walked.

Near the back door we could see the crumpled body of someone on the floor.

"It's that drunk, Two Shots," he told us, stepping to one side so we could see. "He's dead."

Sure enough. On the floor was Two Shots lifeless body. Next to his body was the cross that used to sit on the pulpit, covered with blood.

Someone had used it to bash in his skull, and that someone appeared to be Della DuPont who Harry had grabbed last night coming out of the church.

"Reverend, will you see to it that Two Shots is brought to the undertakers? Harry and I will stop by there later, okay?" Tom said.

"Sure will, sheriff," he told Tom.

"Come on Harry. Let's go back to the office. We can send out for some food. I have a lot to tell you and it is obvious you have a lot to tell also."

"I was just going to suggest the same thing," Harry told Tom. "Come on Carl, let's all go back."

"I'll put some more coffee on," Tom said as they entered the office.

"I'll start, knowing you are all wondering who and why I have a woman locked up in the jail," Harry said.

"Last night, as I went looking for you, Tom, I found out a couple more things. First was the piano player's name who turned out to be Tony. Could his full name be Tony Wright, I don't know. Next. Two Shots name was Ben Horn. He was the older brother to Kellie Horn, who was one of the killer's first victims."

"That was the same information I was able to find out, including Tony's last name. It is Wright," Tom informed them. "He and his sister disappeared the same time his mom and dad were found dead and were never heard from again."

Before anything more was said, the office door opened and a distraught Rosy entered.

"Oh good! You're here," she said. "One of my girls is missing!"

"Calm down," Harry told her. "She might not be missing at all."

His statement drawing the attention of all.

About the same time, the voice of a woman came out of the back room where Harry had Della locked up.

"Who's the girl that's missing?" Harry asked Rosy.

"It's my new girl, Della DuPont," she told him. "She disappeared last night."

"I have Della in my cell back there," Harry told her. "Picked her up last night behind the church."

"You do! What's she done? Can I see her, Harry?" Rosy asked.

"Sure. But I think you will be surprised when you do. Why don't you ask her what she was doing at the church last night, and while you're at it, see what she knows about the drunk everyone knows as Two Shots?"

"Why would you think she knows anything about him? She's new to town by a couple of days and I don't let Two Shots into my place."

"Two Shots was found a short time ago with his head bashed in at the church that I grabbed her from last night. I need to know what, if anything, she might have seen or known concerning him."

Della entered the jail room and Harry closed the door behind her giving them some privacy, hoping this would help in getting Della to talk. Having closed the door, he returned to the discussion he was having with Tom and Carl.

"So, Tom. Were you able to get the sister's name?" Harry asked, hoping he was able to.

"Yes I was, Harry. They were Emma and Della. The only thing is, no one could tell me which one was buried in the grave the day the mother and father were found dead in the root cellar."

Pouring a coffee and offering Carl and Harry one, Tom continued.

"The mother and father were Willard and Irene Wright. The family moved here from back east someplace. They just dropped in out of nowhere it seems."

The cell room door opened and Rosy came out. She was very upset and headed for the office door, stopping only to tell Harry that Della was ready to talk when he was ready, and she had a lot to tell. After saying that, Rosy was gone.

The three of them just stood there. The only movement in the room being Carl's hand as he was writing just as fast as he could.

"Let's get her out here," Tom finally said and headed for the cell room door.

"No," Harry told him, "Not yet. You need to finish your story first."

"Okay," he said. "Where was I? Oh, I remember," he said and continued.

"As I was saying, the Wright's came from nowhere. The farmhouse used to be owned by Ned Cooper, his wife and their two children. One day they were there, the next, they were gone, and the Wright's were there in their place."

"What happened to them?" Harry asked. "They couldn't just disappear? Someone must know where they went."

"No one does, Harry. They just disappeared into thin air."

"Maybe it's time to get Della out here," Tom said again.

"Where were you last night? I looked all over for you, asked around and no one had seen you," Harry said.

"Well, Harry, I went out to the Wright farm and staked it out from the hiding place we discovered in the tree line, but no one came around. I thought I heard some noise in the underbrush but didn't see anything."

Well then, maybe Della can fill in some blanks. Bring her out here, Tom," Harry said.

When Della walked out from the cell room, Harry noticed a completely different look to her face. Gone was the defiant demeanor, replaced by one scared look.

"Would you like a coffee or something to eat?" Harry asked.

Della, just shook her head.

"Take a seat then," Harry told her. "I have some questions for you."

Once she was seated, he began.

"Start by telling us your full name, and it's time to tell the truth. You know you're in a lot of trouble here," Harry told her. "You were at the scene of Two Shots murder."

"I'm not doing this any longer, Harry. I will tell you everything you want to know, starting with my name. It is Della Wright. Tony is my brother and he is the person who killed Two Shotss along with the four whores that have been killed."

Hanging her head, she said in a quiet voice.

"I had nothing to do with his killing, Two Shots, or any other killings."

A moment of silence, a large sigh, and then a confession.

"I did help Tony kill our mother and father after we found our sister dead in the root cellar. They had beaten her to death, so we killed them both, buried our sister, and disappeared. It wasn't till after I received a telegram from Tony, I decided to return."

Harry noticed how quiet the room had become while she told a story that had them all mesmerized.

Where was this story going? Harry wondered.

"Can I have some water, Harry?" she asked.

Tom sat a glass of water in front of her, then we all waited for her to continue.

"I don't know what happened to the Coopers, but I suspect my parents had something to do with them leaving. Maybe even my brother. He was becoming more like our dad as far as his beating us girls. Tony started taking a liking to whipping Emma and me just like our father used to do. But don't misunderstand me, Tony received his share of those beatings too, but more from our mom. She would do to Tony what our dad would do to us girls. She was the one who came up with the idea to brand us. Sometimes she would…."

The office door opened and in walked the mayor, cutting short Della's statement.

"Harry! I heard you…," before he could finish, Harry stopped him.

"Sorry mayor, but I need you to leave," Harry told him and stepped out from behind his desk, and placing his hand on the mayor's shoulder, turned him around and back out the door.

"I'll see you later, but right now isn't the time. I need to go back inside."

Harry went back into the office and left the mayor standing on the boardwalk, bewildered.

"Sorry about that. You can continue now," hoping the interruption by the mayor hadn't effected the moment. It hadn't.

Della had carried a lot of weight on her shoulders and was finally getting rid of it. She had suffered at the hands of her brother also. He would take pleasure in whipping her and Emma, and sometimes he would cut them. After a couple of hours, there was only one more question to be asked.

"Where is Tony now?" was his last question.

"I don't know where he hides during the day, but he will be at the church, tonight. We have been meeting there these past couple of nights. He is everywhere like a ghost! He will know by now you have me. He was right in front of me, last night. A couple of seconds earlier you would have had him. He probably watched everything from behind that large rock that was there."

"You really think he will return to the church?" Harry questioned.

"If you release me, yes. He will be there because he will know I will be, and he will want to know what, if anything, I told you," she continued. "He is tired also. He doesn't mean to harm those women, he just can't stop. Something broke inside of him he can't fix. He becomes a vicious, crazed, rabid animal once he starts. Except he also enjoys it. He told me so."

"I know. We have all seen what he is capable of doing to a person," Harry said in a quiet voice.

Silence filled the room. They had heard Della's story and the quietness was almost like a memorial to those who had suffered and died at her brother's hands.

"Well, Della. I hope you're right. I'm letting you go in hopes he is watching and will meet you at the church tonight. Hopefully, he will show up and we can finally end all this killing."

It would be a long shot he'd show, but the only one they had at the moment. Della left and Harry asked Carl to leave also. Harry needed time with Tom to plan for the evening.

"I'll see you here in the morning," he said, then added, "good luck tonight."

"Thanks Carl, see you in the morning."

Once Carl left, Harry asked Tom if he wanted to go eat as Harry's stomach was growling. Accepting his invite for food, they headed towards Sally's.

Almost immediately after leaving the office, the short hairs on the back of Harry's neck stood up. Instead of feeling threatened, Harry welcomed the feeling knowing the bait was being taken. Heading back to the office later that day, Harry didn't get those same feelings of being watched, so he figured Tony was gone to wherever he went to hide out. He couldn't go play piano anymore.

Tom and Harry only spent a short time in the office. Harry felt they needed to get to the church and settle in for a long wait hoping that he would show up.

Harry had made a comfortable spot behind the pulpit where he also had a good view of the back door. There was just enough moonlight coming into the church where it was possible to see if someone entered.

Tom was sitting on the floor between two rows of benches with a view of the front door, although they figured he wouldn't come in that way. It was more to prevent his exiting.

It had to be somewhere around one o'clock. Harry's eyelids were growing weary, so Harry guessed Tom's must be doing the same, when Harry heard a small creaking sound and saw the back door being opened.

Harry had his pistol in hand, but not cocked.

Della, who was still dressed as a man, slowly entered the church. As instructed earlier, she called out her brother's name.

Getting no response from him, but alerting them, she made her way to the back of the church where she climbed the ladder that went to the bell tower where she told us she had met Tony before and was the location they were to meet again.

Now the trap was set. All that remained was for Tony to take the bait.

Come on Tony. Harry said to himself. Again, hoping against hope he would show up so his reign of terror on the Painted Ladies of Cinnamon Hollow could come to an end.

It was only a matter of minutes after Della had entered that Harry heard the familiar creaking of the door being opened once again. The outline of a man appeared and quickly headed for the back of the church and to the bell tower where he knew his sister was waiting. Harry was already up and headed in his direction, blocking his exit from where he had come in.

To his surprise, Tom's figure came rushing across the room, took a flying leap, and tackled the figure. Both making a loud thud as they hit the floor, but with Tom on top. And just like that, no shots being fired, the reign of terror against the Painted Ladies of Cinnamon Hollow, came to an end.

The End

Epilogue

With the capture of Tony Wright, the town of Cinnamon Hollow breathed a sigh of relief.

Once again, the town's people felt secure and safe.

Although Harry was given much praise for his capture, he made it known, it was only through Tom's excellent actions that it was made possible. Because of the brutality of the killings, there was little hope for Tony when he went to trial.

The guilty verdict was shortcoming, with the sentence of being hanged by the neck until dead was carried out.

There was no saving him. No scaffold was built to carry out the sentence, instead, a limb from the old oak tree which, by the way, acted as a reference marker to one of the many paths he had used to carry out his abductions, was used.

The whole town was there to watch as the wagon on which he stood in was drawn out from under him. Watched as he took that last step into thin air. No free fall and broken neck ending in sudden death the scaffold would have provided, but the slow strangulation he endured as the weight of his body slowly tightened the noose around his neck. He was not even granted a hood, so everyone could see his face as he struggled for breath.

They watched as blood flowed from his nose and ears. Watched as his eyes grew larger and pop from their sockets. The townspeople watched as his feet gave their last twitch before succumbing in death. The whole town cheered that day, all except Tom, Della, and Harry.

As happy inside as Harry was in ending Tony's killing spree, Harry was also saddened by Tony's life ending, leaving a sister in the world to fend for herself. Harry's assignment was over and time now to head for home and his Amanda. Tom was grateful for Harry's offer to become a US Marshal but wanted to stay as sheriff of Cinnamon Hollow.

Harry had noticed him and Della were becoming close. He was by her side during Tony's trial and there for his hanging. Harry felt happy for them both, knowing that healing was needed and having each other, well, the healing might be short lived.

Carl would write an excellent story for the paper, but more so, an excellent book. He would go on to become a great writer of western stories of the wild, wild West.

And as Harry stated earlier, he returned to his lovely wife Amanda, who by the way, told him she was pregnant with their first child.

As the times changed, Harry was able to change her mind and they moved to a bigger city.

One with a train station….